For Sara Lundberg, who keeps climbing down in the trenches with me. Your friendship and faith in me means more than you'll ever know.

BRIMSTONE BURGLAR

A RILEY CRUZ NOVEL: BOOK TWO

L.A. MCBRIDE

NEWSLETTER SIGNUP

Subscribe to my newsletter for updates, announcements, contests, and bonus content: lamcbride.com/newsletter/

FOREWORD

This series takes place in the same world as the Kali James series. Each series can be read independently. Although every effort has been made to avoid major spoilers, the events in this book overlap with those of Kali's series and include some shared details.

CHAPTER 1

There's nothing like being drenched in synthetic deer urine to make a girl rethink her life choices. My idea of hunting typically involved rich marks and magical artifacts, so this morning's adventure was a first. I glanced down at my head-to-toe camo and grinned. At least I'd dressed the part.

September in Kansas meant the sun was still hugging the horizon at seven in the morning. After having Helen drop me off by Clinton Lake, I waded through the tall grass. This area served as prime deer hunting grounds every fall. It didn't take long for me to scent my quarry because he smelled as bad as I did.

I approached from downwind, which allowed me to get within forty yards of his perch. I mentally patted myself on the back for being able to sneak up on the man. When Nash Mitchell spotted me, I gave him my best beauty pageant wave. Instead of waving back, the jerk shot an arrow into the ground inches from my boot.

"Hey!" I yelled, scrambling back far enough I hoped I was out of range before holding up a finger. "No," I said firmly.

Nash nocked another arrow and raised his bow. I had to squint to make out his expression. He camouflaged himself far better than I did. Of course, he'd spent years as a Green Beret before his forced early retirement, so he should be better at it. Under all that war paint, he didn't seem happy to see me. I took another giant step back to be safe.

I'd been hounding him for the last month to join my crew, and despite my best attempts, the man had yet to thaw toward me. Maybe I should've expected the arrow since he'd threatened to shoot me the last time I'd dropped by that run-down museum he called home. As far as I could tell, the man spent his days hoarding military paraphernalia, drawing rudimentary chalk circles, and plotting ways to trap demons. Nash Mitchell could use a side order of fun in his life, and I was just the woman to deliver it.

He also had a skill set I needed, which was why I was determined to hire him. A few weeks ago, I couldn't scrounge together enough money for a plane ticket. And look at me now—ready to contribute to the local economy by recruiting a grumpy ex-soldier.

I held my hands up in the universal sign of surrender. "Give me ten minutes," I coaxed.

Nash lowered the bow with an exaggerated sigh and gestured for me to approach. I wasn't an idiot though, so I waited until he hung the weapon from the hook on his tree stand before moving any closer. I tightened the straps on my backpack and then jumped to grab a low branch, pulling myself up to settle next to him.

I tried flattery first. "Nice shot."

He grunted.

This is going well. I scanned the area. There wasn't a deer in sight. I wondered how long he'd been sitting up here. That tree stand couldn't be comfortable. "You know, if you come work for me, you can afford to buy your meat at the grocery store instead of hunting for your supper."

He turned to me with narrowed eyes. "I like to hunt."

I shrugged. As a goat shifter, I couldn't relate to the prey drive that spurred men like Nash into kitting themselves out with weapons and gear just to sit in a tree for hours waiting for a deer.

I eyed the bow. "Wouldn't a rifle be easier?"

"And louder." He looked away. "Besides, the bow is more sporting."

I recognized a haunted look when I saw it, no matter how quickly he covered it. In the last couple of weeks, I'd done a lot of research on Green Berets and the missions they were sent on. "I'm sure the deer will be happy to hear that," I teased, trying to lighten the mood.

"Say your piece and then get lost, kid." He gave me the once over. "You're scaring away the wildlife."

I huffed. "How am I scaring away the wildlife?" I put scaring in air quotes and pointed to my outfit. "I dressed to blend in."

Nash snorted.

"What? I did." I shopped at a hunting store yesterday and everything. In addition to the camo, I was now the proud owner of a tricked-out pocketknife packed with gadgets like a bottle opener and a fire starter. I couldn't wait to try both options out.

"Sure. That pink hair blends right in." Nash shook his head. "Now say what you got to say, so I can tell you no again, and you can leave."

"Don't you want more excitement in your life than sitting in a tree hoping some poor deer wanders by?"

"No." He made a shooing motion.

I wasn't giving up that easily. When I made no move to leave, Nash pulled his green camo cap off and slapped it on my head with another exaggerated sigh.

"Thanks!" I adjusted it so it didn't block my view.

"How did you know where to find me?"

"Your neighbor Harold told me." One pastry bribe and a bit of sweet talking, and Harold was more than happy to tell me all about Nash's weekend plans. He even drew me a handy dandy map.

"That reminds me." I swung my backpack around and dug out the paper bag I'd picked up before catching a ride over here. With a happy inhale, I pulled out a still-warm cinnamon roll. It smelled divine. Even though my stomach protested handing it over, I offered it to Nash.

He stared at it. "You brought a cinnamon roll deer hunting?"

"I thought you might be hungry." I waved the roll under his nose with one hand while licking a smear of frosting off my other hand.

"I can't eat that," he bit out, looking at the roll with disgust.

"Are you diabetic or something?"

"What? No." Nash grabbed the roll out of my hand and stuffed it in the paper bag before shoving it in my backpack.

"Are you one of those health nuts who hates sugar?" That would explain his surly attitude.

"I'm trying to hunt."

"So?"

"So, that thing reeks. It's going to scare away the deer."

"Because deer are afraid of cinnamon rolls?" I asked skeptically.

Instead of answering, Nash closed his eyes and counted to ten. He wasn't the first man to do so in my presence, and he probably wouldn't be the last.

So much for my peace offering. I thought of the sad, smooshed cinnamon roll. He didn't deserve it, anyway. *More for me.* I tried to dig it out again, but Nash slapped my hand and glared.

I threaded my ponytail through his hat and tried a different angle. "You know, I looked up the monthly payout amount for veteran's disability checks." I didn't let his grunt dissuade me. "It's shit." I wasn't lying. The amount might put my previously meager bartender wages to shame, but it didn't allow for much more than subsistence living. "If you come work for me, I'll give you twenty-five percent. That's twenty-five grand a job—every dollar of it under the table."

When the Enclave offered me the gig to retrieve demon artifacts, I'd negotiated a fat commission plus all expenses paid. I'd already offered Dez twenty-five percent to provide tech support, but I needed the kind of muscle and skill Nash Mitchell would bring to the team. I eyed his scraggly blond beard and sun-weathered hands. This was definitely a man who knew how to blow some shit up.

As I'd hoped, dangling that much money got his attention. Those pretty hazel eyes of his locked on mine. "How old are you, kid? Twenty-one?"

I gritted my teeth against the nickname. "It's Riley. Not kid. And I'm twenty-five," I countered. I'd recently celebrated my birthday with Alyce's homemade death-by-chocolate cake and a raucous night of karaoke at my favorite dive bar.

Based on the dismissive shake of his head, the extra four

years didn't impress him. "Who's dumb enough to pay a twenty-five-year-old kid a hundred grand to steal demon artifacts?" he scoffed.

I narrowed my eyes. By now, he knew I hated being called kid, which meant he was being a dick on purpose. "Stop calling me kid."

"Stop stalking me." He turned back to stare at the empty field where there were still no deer.

I circled back to the money. "The who doesn't matter. All that matters is that they're willing to pay top dollar for us to play fetch."

He was human, which meant I wouldn't be telling him about the supernatural governing body known as the Enclave until he was officially Team Riley. It was bad enough Nash knew supernaturals existed, but thanks to his tinnitus, he couldn't be compelled to forget about us. Dez tried. Since Nash already knew about the things that went bump in the night, I could recruit him for my heist crew without breaking the cardinal rule of secrecy in our world.

"I'm willing to give you an advance. Ten percent up front and all the shiny weapons your little Rambo heart desires." I nudged his shoulder. "Come on. What do you say? I'll get you a grenade launcher."

"It's still a no."

"If you won't do it for the money, then do it for the chance to screw over some demons."

The man fancied himself a demon hunter. If he worked with me, at least he could channel that aggression into something that wouldn't be a guaranteed death sentence. Being a badass special forces dude was one thing, going up against demons was another. He wouldn't live to see forty-three if he kept baiting demons on his own.

I held my breath when he didn't immediately say no. For the first time since I started recruiting him, I could tell he was actually considering it.

"I'll share everything I know about demons." I promised. Then I dangled the carrot I knew he couldn't resist. "Plus, I know a computer guy who can hack into anything." Maybe not anything, but with enough time and incentive, Dez could definitely hack into classified government files—like the one on Nash's last black op. "Do one job with me on a trial basis, and I'll have him pull the file on that Peru op that ended your military career," I offered.

He stiffened. "Stealing artifacts is illegal," Nash pointed out. It wasn't a no.

I had him. "You don't seem like the kind of guy who's afraid of breaking a few laws for a good cause."

Before he could shut me down again, my cell phone blasted out The Struts' "Dirty Sexy Money," telling me exactly who was calling. *Finally.* While I dug out my phone, Nash snatched his hat off my head, jumped down, and started packing up his gear.

I looked down at him. "I thought you were hunting."

Nash lunged for my leg and yanked me out of the tree. Luckily, I was good at landing on my feet.

I waved the still ringing phone in my hand. "Our first job."

"I didn't agree to do a job," he argued.

Ignoring him, I answered the phone. "Hi Sato. What do you got for me?"

"Not over the phone. Meet me at Volkov's house in an hour for instructions." The Enclave's errand boy hung up before I could object to meeting at the local alpha's house.

With a groan, I tucked the phone back in my pocket. Then I pasted on a big smile. "It looks like I need a ride. Duty calls."

Nash pointed at my phone. "Better call a ride share then."

"Oh, come on. You've got a perfectly good beater sitting in the parking lot. Give me a lift. You can tag along to find out what the job is," I coaxed. "Tell you what, if you don't like what you hear, you can walk, and I'll leave you alone."

A muscle twitched in his cheek, but he reached up to remove his deer stand from the tree. "This doesn't mean I'm taking the job."

I grinned. He was totally taking the job, even if he wasn't ready to admit it yet.

CHAPTER 2

$\mathcal{N}$ash parked in front of Volkov's house, making sure to angle his beat-up truck so it blocked the view from the oversized library windows where the alpha stood glaring at us. I wasn't in a hurry to get out of the truck.

Max Volkov and I had struck something of a truce during my last job. I'd been dodging him just the same. I knew I couldn't avoid the post I-saw-you-naked awkwardness forever, but that didn't mean I was ready to deal with it either.

When I remained sitting, Nash poked his head back in the truck. "Don't get cold feet on me now, kid."

I squared my shoulders and climbed out, meeting Volkov's narrowed gaze through the window as I walked toward his front door. I wondered if the dirty look was for me for avoiding him or for my scruffy sidekick. *Only one way to find out.* I didn't bother knocking.

Nash followed me inside, his eyes cataloging exits in much the same way Volkov did when he entered a room. The two men had a lot more in common than they'd ever admit. Maybe if Nash hadn't broken into my apartment and taken pot shots at Volkov while escaping through the alley, the two of them might have been friendly. As it was, Volkov wasn't the forgiving type.

The alpha headed us off in his spacious entryway, braced for a fight. Even dressed in a perfectly pressed business suit, Max Volkov radiated barely leashed violence. And—if I was honest—a whole lot of sex appeal. *Nope. Not going there. This is business.*

"What's he doing here?" Although Volkov directed the question to me, he never took his eyes off Nash, but he grimaced when he got a whiff of us. "And why do you both stink?"

"I asked him to come. We were deer hunting." I ignored Nash's snort and tried to edge past Volkov.

Volkov didn't budge, looking skeptical about my newfound hunting interest despite the camouflage I was rocking. He stepped closer, smelling a lot better than we did. The temptation of spiced cedarwood and bad choices wrapped around me as he invaded my personal space. "You won't need him for this."

Despite my best intentions, I leaned into him. "Max, we talked about this." I'd been upfront about my plan to hire Nash.

"I didn't think you'd get him to agree," he admitted. When I took a deep breath and a step back, Volkov flashed Nash a smile over my shoulder that was all teeth. "You can go now. I'll take her home when we're done here."

I turned so I could keep an eye on both of them before things escalated. Instead of bristling as I expected, Nash's whole body relaxed as if the alpha was no more threatening than a toddler. Although Nash carried himself with the self-assurance of a soldier, he was only a couple inches taller than my five-eight with the kind of lean build that allowed him to fade into a crowd. Given his background, there was no doubt he could hold his own in a fight—against humans, anyway—but Max Volkov was used to being the biggest threat in the room. The easy dismissal had Volkov's hackles up. Nash had his number, all right.

Nash held Volkov's gaze as he moved closer to me. "I'm not going anywhere. Riley here needs someone to watch her six." He dropped a heavy arm across my shoulders. "And she chose me for the job."

I groaned, knowing how Volkov was going to react before the growl rumbled up his throat. Volkov's eyes changed from arctic blue to the amber of his wolf.

Undeterred, Nash tugged me closer and tsked. "Feeling territorial there, Benji?"

Normally, I was the one antagonizing Volkov, but today I wasn't in the mood to play wind-up-the-werewolf. I had a job to do, and this little dick measuring contest was wasting time. I shrugged off Nash's arm along with his feigned interest.

"Stop antagonizing him," I warned.

When he opened his mouth to ratchet up the testosterone, I dug my elbow into his side. Nash grunted and dropped his arm.

I turned my attention back to Volkov. "I'm not sure why we're here in the first place, since the job has nothing to do with you." I tilted my head and stared up at him.

Had he pulled the Tribunal card to insert himself into my business? As the head of the governing body of the Interior Territory, Volkov was a certified control freak. But even he answered to the Enclave, and they were the ones employing me. Max Volkov should have nothing to do with any jobs they sent my way.

Volkov stopped glowering at Nash long enough to scan my camouflage-covered body. "Everything that happens in this city is my business," he countered, the heat in his eyes making it clear he included me in that claim.

Nash took in Volkov's buttoned-up business wear and bedroom eyes with a wide grin. "She's too wild for you, man."

Volkov didn't smile back. "She's too young for you."

I rolled my eyes. "I'm too smart for either of your bullshit. Now, let's go." I side-stepped both men and headed into the library.

Kage Sato was waiting for us, along with the Kansas City enforcer, Craig Ward. While Craig was a mountain of a man with a shaved head and eyes like granite, Sato was closer to my size. That didn't make him any less intimidating. Despite his unassuming build and his affinity for skinny jeans, Sato possessed an unnerving stillness that marked him as a predator. Although I had no idea what kind of supernatural Sato was, the fact that he was the mouthpiece for the Enclave ensured he was powerful—something Nash picked up on right away. Unlike his needling of Volkov, Nash inclined his head respectfully toward Sato.

Volkov followed us into the room, pausing long enough to say something to Craig that I didn't catch.

"On it," Craig said. He caught my eye and winked before heading for the door. "Play nice."

Fat chance.

I took a seat on the leather sofa. The minute Volkov's attention wasn't on us, Nash dropped all pretense of flirting. Instead of taking the open spot next to me, he moved behind me, putting his back to the wall.

Sato stared at Nash. "You brought a human?"

Volkov smirked as if he'd won.

I ignored him. "My crew. My way." I repeated the terms we'd agreed on when I'd accepted the Enclave's job offer. Technically, Nash hadn't signed on for the job yet, but I kept that detail to myself.

"Surely, you understand our need for discretion, do you not?" Sato asked with a frown.

Nash answered before I could. "I was a Green Beret. I'm well versed in discretion."

"Hmm. That may be." Sato appeared mildly amused. For a man rumored to be the original Shadow, one of the Enclave's deadliest spies and assassins, a stint in human special forces probably wasn't all that impressive. Sato turned his attention back to me. "However, you're the one we've hired. You can pay him for whatever tasks you like without him knowing the job details."

"That's not how this is going to work." I crossed my arms and shot a pointed look toward Volkov. "I don't do hierarchy. We're a team, which means no one is kept in the dark."

That was how my old alpha Carl ran things, hoarding knowledge like power. More than once, he'd sent me on a job without crucial details, and it almost got me killed. I wasn't going to operate like Carl. As far as I was concerned, anyone who was willing to stick their neck out for me was going in with every bit of knowledge I could arm them with. And if Sato couldn't accept that, I'd walk—even if it meant passing up the kind of money that could change my life.

I waited to see if Sato would go back on his word to let me do these jobs with people I chose. My palms grew sweaty as he kept me waiting, his dark eyes unreadable.

"Very well," he finally conceded. "But he'll need to take a binding magical oath to ensure he keeps our secrets."

I expected Nash to balk, but he stepped around the sofa and nodded.

"Does this mean you're on the team?" I asked.

"It means I'm listening," Nash countered.

I'd count that as a win. My phone pinged with a text from Dez saying he'd arrived. While Sato administered the oath, I jumped to my feet to let Dez in. With his messy ginger hair, khakis, and neatly trimmed beard, Dez was his normal nerdy self.

I sat on the sofa, tugging Dez down beside me. "Dez, this is Kage Sato. He's the Enclave's middleman. And I'm sure you remember Nash."

As soon as the words were out, I regretted them. Dez blanched, probably remembering the black eye Nash gave him. Nash crossed his arms over his chest instead of extending a hand. *Well, this is off to a great start*, I thought.

Sato studied Dez. "Working with a vampire is unwise— even one as seemingly harmless as this one."

Dez's shoulders drooped.

I bristled. "Just because Dez doesn't peacock around like the rest of you doesn't mean he can't handle himself." It was a stretch. Dez went light-headed at the sight of blood, but he was as loyal as they came. I sure as shit wasn't going to let anyone make him feel less than.

Nash mumbled something under his breath about blood-suckers, but Sato held a hand up before I could snap at him. "That's not the point, Riley. We're hunting demon artifacts, and I can't risk a vampire tipping off other demons."

While it was true that vampires were essentially human hosts for weak and mid-level demons, that didn't make every vampire team hellfire. Dez was different.

"Too bad. We're a package deal." I pulled out a piece of

gum and stuck it in my mouth. "If you're worried about it, you can have Dez do your whole magical pinky swear thing."

After a long silence during which Sato tried to intimidate me, Dez fidgeted self-consciously, and I blew cinnamon-scented bubbles with my gum, Sato caved. "Fine."

I sat up straighter. "Great. Now, why don't you tell us what we're stealing?"

Sato frowned. "I'm afraid it's not that simple."

Based on the loaded look he shared with Volkov, I was certain that whatever the complication was, I wasn't going to like it.

CHAPTER 3

The last time I sat in Volkov's well-appointed library with an open book in my lap, it had been the morning after our one-night stand. I examined the book Volkov had just handed me and tried to bury the memory. "What am I looking at?"

Volkov flipped the book open to a marked page, his fingers brushing my thigh. His smile at my sharp inhale said he'd done it on purpose. He pointed to an illustration of a young demon with an angelic face and wicked eyes. Inky black wings spread behind the demon, and fire snakes danced at his feet.

"Your job is to acquire an artifact forged by the demon Valac," Sato said. "Don't let the baby face fool you. Valac is powerful, as is the artifact he created."

I scanned the text under the picture. "According to this, he's capable of commanding serpents and can bestow the ability to control other people on those who summon him." I flipped the page, but there wasn't much else about the demon.

I handed the book back to Volkov and turned to Sato. "What's the artifact?"

"It's an object that he imbued with the power to control others."

Dez and I exchanged a glance. He asked the question I was thinking. "Why would an artifact like that be any more dangerous than your run-of-the-mill vampire?"

Like their full-blooded counterparts, vampires had the power to compel others—supernaturals and humans alike. As far as I knew, there were only two exceptions, and we were both in this room. For whatever reason, I'd always been immune to both vampire compulsions and alpha commands. And thanks to his tinnitus, compulsions had no effect on Nash, either. We hadn't tested the alpha command yet to see if we also had that resistance in common. Volkov was going to lose his shit if he couldn't boss Nash around.

Sato shook his head. "Control, not compel," he corrected.

"What's the difference?" Nash asked before I could.

"The difference is that vampires can compel people to do something specific. They can block a recent memory or compel an action. The object Valac made allows the wielder to completely take over the will of another—to turn anyone into their thrall."

I shivered. The idea of someone with the power to turn a person into a living, breathing puppet was terrifying. No wonder the Enclave was anxious to take an artifact like that out of circulation. "What's the artifact?"

Sato grimaced. "We don't know."

I leaned forward. "What do you mean, you don't know?" How was I supposed to steal something without knowing what it was?

"There's a vague mention of Valac's artifact in our texts, but there's not a description or illustration," Sato admitted.

"How many of these artifacts are there?" Nash asked.

"Dozens, most likely," Sato said. "We've had to comb through the demon texts for mentions of them, but we don't have a complete listing."

Dozens of demon artifacts meant job security, and at the amount they were paying me, I would be a rich woman before hide-and-seek was over. "Where is this mystery artifact?" With any luck, it would be in Hawaii, so I could get the Enclave to pay for an all-inclusive beach vacation and call it a job-related expense.

Sato interrupted my daydreaming. "About a month ago, the Enclave got a tip that the artifact had surfaced in a small village in the Yukon." Sato paused, watching my reaction. A month was a long time to sit on a tip.

I blew another bubble and waited for the rest.

"We sent a more seasoned retrieval specialist after it," Sato admitted.

I rolled my eyes at Sato's wordsmithing. A thief was a thief, no matter how you prettied up the job title. Until now, I had naively thought I was the only retrieval specialist the Enclave employed. Having professional competition was going to eat into my profits.

"Let me guess," Nash said. "Your retrieval specialist took off with it."

"That's one possibility," Sato admitted. "We know he secured the artifact because he reported in on schedule. However, instead of meeting at our arranged rendezvous point, he called to report a delay. That was a week ago and the last we heard from him."

"If you have access to his cell records, then you should be able to pinpoint his location," Dez reasoned.

"Right after the call, the signal went dark," Sato said. "Either he destroyed it, or someone caught up to him."

Dez pulled his phone out, opened the notes app, and went into computer sleuth mode. "I'll need his name and number to track him."

"I'm afraid I'm not authorized to disclose that information." Sato didn't seem happy about it.

"Okay," Dez said. "Forget the name. All I need is the phone number."

"I'm not—"

"Authorized," Dez finished with irritation.

"What makes you think he was in Kansas City?" Nash asked. It was a good question. Kansas City was a long way from the Yukon.

"His last check-in call didn't come from his cell phone," Sato said. "He called from a pay phone outside a biker bar on Prospect."

I leaned forward. "Wait. Businesses still have pay phones like it's the eighties?"

"Apparently," Sato said. "And after some deliberation, the Enclave has agreed to send you after the missing artifact."

I bristled. "What deliberation?"

Sato sighed. "It was not a unanimous decision."

Wow. Way to make a girl feel like the A-team. I popped a bubble and swore under my breath. "So, we're basically the cleanup crew," I guessed.

Sato didn't correct me.

"Did your guy make any other calls?" Nash asked.

"I'm not authorized to share that information," Sato said.

Everyone in the room stared at him, Volkov included. "What are you authorized to share?" Volkov asked.

"I've given you all the information I can," Sato said. "The rest is above my paygrade."

"Let me get this straight." I held three fingers up, so I could tick off them off. "You're sending us after an artifact without one, a description, two, a location, or three, the name of the guy who probably screwed you over." At Sato's curt nod, I stretched my arms across the back of the couch, crossed a leg over my thigh, and leveled Volkov with a dark look. "And I suppose you've enlisted the help of Max here to help track your runner down."

All werewolves were good trackers. Max Volkov was exceptional, which no doubt made the fact that I'd been able to evade him last month particularly galling.

"Not exactly," Volkov said. "It seems we've got ourselves yet another rogue witch practicing forbidden magic."

At this point, blood magic was right up there with barbecue as a Kansas City staple. "What makes you think they're connected?" I asked.

"I don't believe in coincidence," Volkov said. "We've uncovered two sites that reeked of blood magic—the first of which we discovered the day after the Enclave's lackey and the demon artifact went missing."

The timing was suspicious. I'd give him that. But because we were meeting in his house about a job the Enclave hired me to do, I suspected this was yet another attempt to take control. He may have backed off his insistence that I join the pack for my own protection, but that didn't mean he would stay out of my business.

"And the other ritual site?" Nash asked.

"The other was reported yesterday. So far, no one's talking," Volkov said.

That explained where Craig was headed. As the Tribunal's enforcer, Craig was the supernatural version of the law for the Interior Territory, which spanned from North Dakota to Oklahoma and as far east as Ohio. Made up of representatives from each of the major supernatural groups—shifters, vampires, witches, and necromancers—the Tribunal stepped in to settle inter-faction disputes and crimes that affected the supernatural community at large. Because Volkov was not only the Kansas City alpha but also head of the Tribunal, he called the shots on cases like this and often waded into investigations.

While most people were smart enough to be wary of both men, Craig had the temperament to question the locals. Volkov ran far too hot for that. Craig would probably have the name of the witch for Volkov by the end of the week. Regardless, the witch wasn't my concern. My job was to procure the missing artifact.

I stood up and stretched before facing Volkov. "Great. If you get any leads on my artifact, let me know. Until then—"

"Until then, you'll be working together," Sato finished. "Volkov will get you up to speed."

"Hell no. I have my team."

Sato tilted his head. "And now you have a partner."

From Volkov's smug expression, I was certain he engineered this. I'd also bet his definition of partner and mine were going to be radically different.

Sato pulled out a brand-new cell phone box, glancing at Dez before handing it to me. "My cell number is the only one programmed in it. Call when you've secured the artifact." He reached in his pocket and pulled out a slip of paper with a number written on it. "This is your new bank account. You'll find fifty percent of your fee has been deposited into the account. The rest—plus incidentals—is payable upon completion. I'll expect itemized receipts for any expenses."

Sato didn't wait around for a response. By the time I recovered enough to follow him out the door, he'd already disappeared. As I scanned the driveway, it occurred to me that Nash's truck and Dez's car were the only vehicles parked there, which meant whatever Sato was, he wasn't dependent on four wheels like the rest of us to make his escape.

CHAPTER 4

As I suspected, Volkov's idea of partnership involved issuing orders. He went straight into alpha-bosshole mode. "You can go," he told Nash.

Apparently, Nash didn't like being told what to do any more than I did. He crossed his arms and leaned against the driver's door of his truck, his message clear. Although Nash technically hadn't agreed to do this job yet, the fact that he didn't ditch me at the first opportunity seemed like a positive sign.

I held up my index finger. "One minute, and I'll be ready to go."

I turned to Dez who'd followed us. "Hey, do you think you could identify the pay phone and hack into the call records? If we could get a list of all the outgoing calls that day, we could find out if our mystery thief called anyone else." I couldn't imagine it being a long list. How many people used a pay phone these days?

Dez nodded. "No problem. I'll text when I have something." Dez was still getting used to my spontaneous hugs, but he barely startled this time. "You want a lift?"

"Nah. I can catch a ride with Nash. I'll give you a call later," I promised.

Volkov spun me around to face him before I made it to Nash's truck. He was a good six inches taller than me, so I took a big step back to avoid talking to his chest. Honestly, the way I smelled, I was doing him a favor. I could barely stand to be around myself. I definitely needed a shower to wash off this stench before I questioned anyone.

"We need to find whoever sold the spell ingredients left at the ritual site." Volkov glared at Nash who still lounged against his truck, watching us. "It doesn't require a human tag-a-long."

I raised a brow. "We? No offense, but that sounds like a you job." Or maybe a Craig job. But definitely not a Riley job. "Listen Max, I have an artifact to locate."

"Which we'll find, but this is our best lead," Volkov insisted.

Sure. If I was searching for the witch. But I was more concerned with hunting down the thief who stole the artifact in the first place, and that meant starting with the pay phone he called Sato from. "Which is why you should go check it out," I said. "Besides, I need a shower."

He angled his body closer and dropped his voice. "As you know, I have a very well-equipped shower." He wasn't lying. That thing had built-in aromatherapy and a sturdy seat perfect for—well, all sorts of things. The hooded eyes sweeping down my body left no doubt he was remembering the last time we were in there.

The sudden image of him under that glorious rainfall showerhead flashed in my memory—his dark head tipped back, rivulets of shampoo gliding over the hard planes of his back. And lower. I fanned the collar of my shirt to cool off before I caught myself and dropped my hand back to my side. *Nope. Not going there.* I needed to get it through my head that it had been a onetime thing and stop reliving the highlight reel.

I ignored his knowing smile. "I need a change of clothes, which means showering at my place."

"Okay," he said. "I'll pick you up at one and buy you lunch at Arthur Bryant's before we head to the coven."

My stomach rumbled. Oh, this man had me figured out, alright. Barbecue was practically my love language. "I say we divide and conquer. We can touch base tomorrow to compare notes," I suggested, looking at Nash, who was now sitting impatiently in the driver's seat. At least, he hadn't honked at me yet. Or left.

Volkov narrowed his eyes. "You heard Sato. Partners."

"About that. I was thinking more relay team, less figure skating kind of partners."

He stared at me. "Figure skating?"

"I just mean that you'll run the witch investigation, and if you find the artifact, you pass the baton to me. Total cooperation. Partners." Before he could argue, I hurried to Nash's truck and opened the passenger door. "I'll take a rain check on that barbecue though!"

As soon as he pulled out of Volkov's driveway, Nash turned on a classic country music station, probably hoping I wouldn't talk over the music.

I bumped the volume down a notch. "So, are you in?"

Nash took so long to answer, I was sure it would be a no. "One job. And you get me that classified report."

"Deal." I sang along to the chorus of a George Strait song, ignoring Nash's pained expression.

Nash shut the radio off before the song ended. "What do you need me to do?" he asked.

I sniffed the air and wrinkled my nose. "I was serious about those showers."

Nash gave me the side-eye but cracked open his window. "And then?"

He asked like he didn't expect me to have an answer for that. "And then we need to find the identity of the missing thief."

"You think you'll get that by calling the numbers your buddy pulls from the pay phone?" He turned onto my street and parked in front of my apartment building.

I tucked my leg under me and turned toward him. "Doubtful. But I have a better idea." I pulled my shiny new cell phone out of its case and tapped on the screen. "Sato might not be authorized to give us their retrieval specialist's number, but I do have his cell number."

"You're going to have Dez hack Sato's cell records to see the incoming calls." Nash sounded mildly impressed.

"Bingo. I'm betting that Sato's contact list is pretty sparse, so there shouldn't be too many numbers to trace. It's possible, of course, that Sato bought our guy a burner like mine, but it's worth a shot." I'd put our odds at fifty-fifty. I'd bet on worse. "If we can find a name for our mystery thief, Dez can get us a photo."

It wouldn't be the first time Dez hacked into the DMV to get a driver's license photo. He'd done it when he was searching for my parents' records. Unfortunately, there hadn't been any records to find. I hadn't realized how desperately I wanted the photos until Dez couldn't find any. It had been a decade since I'd seen my mom and dad. Every family photograph burned to ash in the fire that killed them, and even precious memories faded. At twelve, my parents thought I was too young to have a cell phone, so I didn't even have digital photos. I'd happily take terrible driver's license photos if it meant seeing my parents' faces one more time.

I rubbed the ache in my chest and cleared my throat. "With a photo, we can start asking around," I said.

Nash stared at me. "You want to walk into a biker bar on Prospect, and start asking questions?"

Prospect Avenue had more than its share of murders and violent crime, but I'd been in far more dangerous places. With his background, Nash had, too. "You got a better idea?" I challenged.

He grabbed my new cell phone with a grumble and added his number to the contacts. "Call me when you have a photo, and I'll start earning my cut."

I gave him a thumbs up and got out of the truck, singing "Every Little Honky Tonk Bar" all the way to my door.

CHAPTER 5

$\mathcal{U}$nlike my sketchy neighborhood, Dez lived in a swanky complex complete with a heated pool and a clubhouse. I imagined what it would feel like living in a place like this as I walked from the city bus stop the next afternoon. It wasn't Volkov-level nice, but they had complimentary towels poolside, despite every apartment having a washer and dryer. No feeding your last quarters into a thirty-year-old machine only to discover that it was—once again—out of order. Now that I was on the cusp of pulling down the big bucks, I could entertain the idea of moving out of my run-down apartment with its non-existent water pressure and buzzing fluorescent lights.

I jogged up the stairs to Dez's second-floor apartment. I'd texted Dez on the bus ride over, and he opened the door before I could knock. Even when lounging at home, Dez dressed in khakis and a button-down shirt. I made a mental note to buy him pajama pants for his birthday. I saw some online that he might even wear, the cotton draw-string pants covered in ones and zeros.

Inside Dez's apartment, I kicked my shoes off by the door and plopped onto his overstuffed couch. I loved that he filled his place with creature comforts instead of the sterile glass and metal that made up so many tech spaces. When I got the paycheck from the Enclave for this job, I was definitely going to buy a new comfy couch like his. I'd even pay to have it delivered.

Dez grabbed his laptop and settled in beside me.

"Any luck?" I asked.

"Luck has nothing to do with what I do," he boasted, pulling up a document with a list of names and numbers. "The pay phone is outside a dive bar called Boondocks that caters to bikers."

I pointed out a familiar number. "This one is the number Sato gave me." I scanned the list. "Did you have time to check the others out?"

Dez nodded. "Most of the outgoing calls were to local businesses. One of them was to a seventy-year-old who lives in Merriam."

"You said most."

Dez pointed to a number with a 705 area code. "This one is an Ontario phone number, and the call was made within minutes of the call to Sato."

"As in Canada?" I asked. "Wouldn't that be an expensive call to make from a pay phone?"

"I assume so."

"There's no name by that number," I pointed out.

"That's because it's a prepaid that was purchased from a Toronto store using cash," he said.

The Ontario connection was still good information, even if I didn't know what it meant. Hopefully, my next ask would end in more actionable intel. "Can you pull the call logs for Sato's number?"

"Sure. What are you thinking?"

"I'm thinking the thief who went missing probably used that cell number that Sato isn't authorized to give us."

Dez smiled. "Which means it's probably a traceable number."

"Exactly."

While Dez got to work, I wandered into his kitchen to get snacks. Technically, Dez didn't need to eat. As a vampire, blood was enough to sustain him. But like his clothes and the black-framed glasses he still wore, Dez held on to the things that made him feel human. His snack cabinet was fully stocked. I grabbed a bag of pretzels and two glasses of water before heading back to the couch.

Dez was a certifiable tech wizard, and he had a name and photo printed on glossy paper within the hour. Luca Cardelli was a thirty-six-year-old with a baby face and a New York address. Because Cardelli made both pay phone calls around five in the afternoon, I was hoping the bar's regulars might be able to ID him. It was a little after two now. I called Nash with the address and told him to meet me there at a quarter to five.

"Be careful," Dez warned after I hung up. "Boondocks is in a rough area with bad lighting and no security cameras. It's not the kind of place that welcomes questions."

"I'll be fine, Dez." Rough or not, it was a human bar. I might not have Volkov's strength, but I was a shifter, with all the perks that came with that.

"I can take you," Dez offered, his warm brown eyes worried.

I loved that he offered, but guys who looked like Dez didn't step foot in a place like that. Plus, he drove a tiny, fuel-efficient smart car. The second he parked it in the lot next to all those Harleys, we'd guarantee a hostile reception.

"I appreciate the offer, but there's a bus stop a couple blocks away. The ride will give me time to think through my questions. Besides, I'm not going alone. I'll have Nash with me."

Dez rubbed the back of his neck. "Just be careful."

I knew he was still worried despite letting the topic drop, so I gave him a distraction. "I do have something else I need your help with. It's not urgent, but can you dig into that last op Nash Mitchell was sent on?"

He raised a brow. "Peru?"

"That's the one."

Dez's eyes lit up. "That'll require breaking into classified files."

"If you're up for it," I teased.

Dez clutched his chest like I'd mortally wounded him.

I slapped his shoulder. "You're really embracing this whole cyber-crime thing. I'm afraid I've corrupted you."

Dez chuckled. "You think this is my first government hacking job?"

"Isn't it?"

Dez smiled. "That's a story better told over cocktails."

Since quitting my job as a bartender at the Sundowner, Dez and I had a standing Thursday night cocktail hour at my place. He supplied the ingredients, and I mixed the Bloody Mary cocktails spiked with the O positive he loved. Sometimes, Kali would join us, and we'd all watch campy old movies. Other times, it would just be Dez and I talking until the early morning hours. No matter how we spent it, Thursday had quickly become my favorite night of the week.

I bumped his shoulder with mine. "I'll hold you to that."

Dez grew serious. "There's something else, unrelated to all of this, that I wanted to show you." He opened a new document on his laptop and motioned me closer.

I popped another pretzel in my mouth and stared at the screen. "What am I looking at?"

"It could be nothing," he warned. "But you remember how you had me dig into those deposits into Carl's bank account?"

I'd asked Dez to check into a series of deposits made to Carl's bank account prior to him becoming the alpha of the Santa Fe pack. I wanted to know who had bankrolled Carl's power grab, and Dez had delivered. "Yeah. You traced them back to Damien Creed." I wasn't sure where he was going with this.

Dez ran his finger down the list of numbers, pausing on each deposit to make sure I noticed them. "The deposits were all the same amount at regular intervals, right?"

"Right."

"And they stopped the night of the fire."

The night my parents died in that fire. I swallowed past the sudden lump in my throat.

Dez glanced at me to ensure I was holding it together before continuing his explanation. "When you asked me to check into those deposits, I found the pattern here." He pointed to another transaction. "Because they were identical amounts, it was easy to do a search to find all of them."

"Makes sense."

He looked up from the laptop. "It does, but because I only searched for that one amount, I missed something. There was one more big deposit into Carl's account." Dez scrolled through the pages until he came to one with a highlighted number. "This one was for five times the amount of the previous deposits. And it happened years after the others stopped." He pointed at the date next to the sum.

I sucked in a breath and slouched back in my seat. That date was branded into my memory. It was the day my old alpha Carl handed me the opportunity to ditch him and the screwed-up pack he led. "That's the day he decided to go after the chip of the Alatyr stone Creed was going to auction off."

Carl had chased rumors of that artifact for years. And in all the years since, his obsession with that stone hadn't lessened. He'd left me two threatening voicemails just last week, demanding I return his stone—or else.

No way was it a coincidence that Carl announced we were going after the Alatyr stone on the same day he came into that windfall. I stared at the number, all the possibilities of what it might mean running through my head. Only one thing was certain. "There's no chance that Damien Creed paid Carl to steal from himself."

Dez smiled approvingly. "You're right. That deposit didn't come from Creed."

Someone must have paid Carl to take it. "Who sent it?" This could be what I needed to bury Carl. If I found out who paid him off, I could pass the info to Creed, and he'd take matters into his own hands.

"It took me awhile to trace it because the money was routed through multiple accounts before landing in Carl's bank," Dez said. "But that deposit came from Zara Bellarose."

I covered my mouth with my hand and looked between Dez and the highlighted number on the screen, my pulse racing. "You're sure?" I asked.

"Positive," he said with a broad grin that rivaled my own. "That's not all." He scrolled to a second identical number in the withdrawal column. "She took the money back a month later."

"Probably when Carl realized he wasn't going to find me." I jumped up and started pacing, unable to sit still. "You know what this means, right? Bellarose paid Carl to go after the Alatyr stone, to steal it from Damien Creed. And when Carl couldn't deliver, she took her money back." I stopped abruptly and stared at Dez. "When Creed finds out, Carl's a dead man."

This find was better than I could've hoped for. The weight I'd been carrying on my chest since Carl found me in Kansas City lifted. Dez barely had time to set his computer aside before I threw my arms around him in a bear hug. He'd just handed me my freedom, and with it, the power to destroy Carl.

All I had to do was get this information in Creed's hands. He'd do the rest. Carl would get what was coming to him, and I wouldn't have to live with his blood on my hands.

CHAPTER 6

Turns out, I was half right. At least fifty percent of the people in this biker bar were human. I also spotted three guys I was pretty sure were vamps, a witch I'd seen around, and a shifter I'd served when I bartended at the Sundowner. Whether human or supernatural, everyone in the place adhered to the same dress code. I'd never seen this much black leather and beards congregated in one room.

Between Nash's wild man appearance and my ripped jeans and leather jacket, we looked like regulars. That worked in our favor. While everyone gawked at us when we walked in the dimly lit bar, no one appeared outright hostile. That would probably last right up until the first question rolled off my lips.

Nash ordered us each a bottle of domestic beer. While the bartender grabbed them, Nash bent his head close to mine. "We're going to ease into this. Just stand there, drink your beer, and let me do the talking."

I snorted. I didn't bring Nash along for his verbal skills.

The bartender removed the caps and set the ice-cold

bottles in front of us. He was human, as far as I could tell, but the man was massive, and not in a bodybuilder sort of way. He had to be at least six and a half feet tall with a long beard and a belly that bumped the bar when he handed us our drinks.

It was a few minutes after five, and while there were a dozen people in here, it wasn't crowded yet. That meant, there was no one clambering for another drink. I pulled the picture out of my pocket before he moved away. His expression went from apathetic to combative faster than I could slide it across the bar.

"Have you seen this guy?" I asked, undeterred.

The bartender leaned into the bar, glaring at me without looking at the photo. "I ain't seen shit."

His booming voice caught the attention of everyone around us, and the conversations died. Nash tensed beside me, swearing under his breath. The hair prickled on the back of my neck. I didn't have to turn around to know they were all watching us. Nash picked up the photo and handed it back to me, then jerked his head toward the door.

I slapped the photo back on the bar top. "Let's try this again. Have you seen this guy? Name's Luca," I said his name with a sneer and raised my voice so it would carry. "He swindled my Gran, drained her bank account. She's eighty-fuck-ing-two and lives on social security." I was laying it on thick, but even nasty-tempered bikers had grandmas. I jerked my head toward the front. "He called her from that pay phone out there."

The bartender didn't look down. "I already told you no. Now, get the hell out of my bar."

"We aren't looking for trouble," Nash said. His tone was placating, even as he evaluated the threats in the room.

Nash wrapped his hand around my wrist and tugged. Trouble was exactly what brought us here, and I wasn't leaving without a lead. I broke his hold and tapped the photo again.

The drunk on the barstool next to me squinted at Luca's face. "Looks like a driver's license photo to me," he slurred, tapping his lit cigarette into an empty beer bottle despite the no smoking sign. "How'd ya get that if you don't know this guy?"

The bartender reached for the gun he had stashed under the bar, but he didn't pull it out yet.

I smiled at both men. "That's because my buddy hacked into the DMV to get me that photo." I turned to the drunk. "You seen him? He was here about a week ago."

The man grunted before going back to his beer, and the bartender moved away from his gun. I picked up the photo and put it away, snatching the guy's lighter, so I didn't have to smell his secondhand smoke.

A skinny woman with a moth tattoo and cherry-red lips caught my eye. She looked toward the hallway for the bathrooms and then back at me. I gave her a slight nod and a head start.

"What a waste of time," I bitched, loud enough the bartender heard me. "I need to use the bathroom, and then we can get out of here."

Nash brushed my hip, and I glanced down to see him slip a switchblade into my jean's pocket. "Don't be long," he said.

I appreciated the gesture, but I didn't need his knife. Despite the speculative looks the vamps shot my way, I made it to the bathroom without incident and locked the door behind me. The woman stood to the side of the sink, nervously eyeing the door. She motioned me closer like she was worried about being overheard. I obliged, turning on the faucet for white noise. Between the sound of water and the noise in the bar, no one would hear us unless they had their ears pressed to the door. And if someone was that close, we were screwed, anyway.

I didn't ask her name, and she didn't offer it. Instead, I handed her Luca Cardelli's picture.

"Yeah. I saw him. We don't get many strangers here, so I noticed him right away." She stared at his picture. "I came out for a smoke, and he was talking to someone on that pay phone—your gran, I suppose. He hung up and then made another call. He was on the phone the whole time I was out there."

I sucked in a breath. This was even better information than I'd hoped for. "You heard the conversation, then?"

She nodded. "I caught most of it. He sounded like he was trying to keep it real vague, like he knew I was listening. But I think he was talking to a partner or something. He mentioned knowing someone who specialized in that kind of work. I got the feeling he didn't like whoever it was though."

"What makes you say that?" I asked.

"Well, he said he'd contact the witch," she said. "Maybe he was talking about an ex or something."

Oh, he wasn't talking about an ex. But I wasn't going to correct her assumption. It looked like Volkov was right. Our missing artifact seemed connected to the ritual sites. "Did he come into the bar?"

She glanced back at the door before leaning in closer. "He slipped Lou—that's the bartender—a hundred bucks and asked him where the best place would be to lie low around here."

"What'd Lou say?"

She looked at Cardelli's picture again before handing it

back to me. "Lou took one look at that guy's fancy shoes and told him to head to Overland Park."

I laughed, not expecting that answer, which meant it was good advice. Overland Park was as suburban as it got around here, with a per capita income well above the rest of Kansas and Missouri. "Is there anything else you noticed that could help me track him down?"

"He didn't stick around. Kept looking over his shoulder like he was expecting to get jumped."

"Did you see him leave? Get a look at his car, maybe?" I doubted I'd get that lucky, but I had to try.

"No. Sorry." She worried her lip with her teeth. "If anyone asks—"

"If anyone asks, I'll tell them you told me to get lost," I assured her.

"Thanks." Her shoulders relaxed. "And I'm sorry about your gran. It's a real dick move stealing from a little old lady."

"You got that right," I said, not feeling the least bit guilty about the lie. Given Cardelli's line of work, he'd probably stolen something from a rich little old lady at least once. "Give me five minutes before you come out." I shut off the faucet.

Without the sound of water to buffer us, it didn't take long to realize Nash was in trouble. I'd heard enough bar fights to know what one sounded like.

CHAPTER 7

I came out to complete chaos. Nash had his back to the pool table, where he faced three scary-looking dudes. At least, they all appeared to be human. Nash took the biggest guy out with a shot to the liver. He pivoted to face the next guy, who threw a punch. Nash dodged and shoved the guy's arm across his body, exposing his unprotected side to Nash's fist.

Maybe he has this in hand.

The supernaturals seemed to be following the unwritten rule of staying out of human fights. That didn't mean they were above watching. The witch I'd seen earlier was nowhere to be found, but the vamps were openly cheering Nash's opponents, while the shifter had moved to a bar stool with a better view.

I tried to elbow my way closer, but the trio of vamps stepped in my path.

"I don't think so, Pink." The self-appointed spokesperson for their group eyed me like takeout. "Wouldn't want you to get hurt." The flash of fang belied his concern for my welfare.

I held my hands up. "Fine. I'll stay here."

The sound of a table breaking drew their attention away from me. There was no way I would be getting past them, even with their backs to me. I took advantage of their distraction to jump on top of the bar where I could see, just in time to see Nash take an uppercut to the chin. I winced.

"Aren't you going to do something?" I hollered at Lou, who'd walked out from behind the bar to stand with a group of regulars watching the unfolding brawl.

Lou held up a wad of cash and smiled. That asshole was taking bets.

I sat down on the bar and unlaced one of my combat boots. I watched Nash slam one guy's head into a nearby table before tossing him at his buddies like a human bowling ball. The man could hold his own, but the crowd was circling now, having maneuvered him away from the pool table. I took off a sock. Looking at the happy avocado print, I mourned its loss as I tied it in a knot. I loved these socks, but sometimes sacrifices had to be made.

While Lou was busy rubbernecking, I snatched a bottle of his highest proof vodka and took a healthy swig. It was as bad as Alyce's moonshine. I wasn't normally a hard liquor drinker, but this was about to get ugly. I stood up on the bar again and whistled, bottle still in hand. "Hey! Knock it off!" I yelled.

No one even looked my way—Lou included. Nash already had a fat lip and a gash on his forehead. It was only a matter of time before he went down, and once he was on the floor, he didn't stand a chance. Even if I could fight my way past three vampires, we were outnumbered at least six to one. The time for fists was over.

I doused my sock in alcohol and stuffed it in the bottle, wedging the knot in the neck. I whistled again, this time making it as shrill as I could. Several people looked over at me standing on top of the bar. Once I had their attention, I lit the sock on fire and tossed the bottle on the pool table, throwing it hard enough to shatter. The fire was underwhelming, but it freaked enough people out to cause a stampede for the door.

The vamps were the first to run. Fire tended to send them scampering because it was one of the few ways to kill them. Even the bikers didn't wait around to see what I'd do next. Nash and I were among the last people out of the bar since I had to put my boot back on.

"Nice moves," I told Nash, handing him his switchblade as we walked outside. "For a minute there, I almost thought you had them."

Nash shook his head ruefully. "It's a lot harder to win a fight when you're trying not to kill them."

The bikers clustered together in the Boondocks' parking lot stared as we walked past, but none of them moved to intercept us. Even Lou kept his distance, despite looking like he was ready to blow a gasket. We would have been home free if it wasn't for the livid werewolf stalking toward us.

"You want to do the talking?" I teased Nash, still a bit salty about his whole stand-there-and-look-pretty spiel in the bar.

"Nah," he said. "I think he's less likely to kill you."

I glared at the shifter from the bar, who had obviously called Volkov the minute the fight started, if not sooner. *Scoring brownie points, no doubt.* If he'd actually cared about the outcome, he would've done something other than lean against the bar and sip his beer while watching the fight.

Volkov headed straight for Nash with murder in his eyes. I quickly stepped between them and raised my hands to push Volkov back. He didn't even look down as he grabbed me around the waist and deposited me off to the side.

He stepped up to Nash until the two of them were chest-to-chest. "You're supposed to be keeping her safe, not dragging her into bar brawls," Volkov snarled.

Nash chuckled, as if he had no self-preservation instincts at all. "It looked to me like she can take care of herself."

I wiggled myself between them, braced a hand on each of them, and shoved. Only Nash stepped back. Volkov trapped my hand against his chest and glared at Nash. I tugged my arm until he let go.

Volkov finally looked down at me. "You should've called me. Instead, I had to hear about the fight from one of my guys."

I could tell he was trying to keep his voice calm, so I did the same. "Listen Max, we were outnumbered in there. I needed to break up the fight, and we didn't have time wait around for the cavalry." I spread my arms, gesturing toward the bikers who were still giving me a wide berth. "I handled it."

His eyes flared wide. "You tried to set the bar on fire."

"Pffft. That was barely a fire," I argued. "It's not like I used gasoline."

"You threw a Molotov cocktail on a pool table in a packed bar." He definitely wasn't using his indoor voice now.

"Oh please," I scoffed. "It was hardly packed. The bar's capacity is at least a hundred more than were in there."

He pinched the bridge of his nose. "Not the point."

"No one was in danger. I tossed it on a pool table directly under an indoor fire sprinkler," I countered. "Everyone's fine."

Volkov cooled off enough to scan the people milling around the parking lot. "Maybe so, but it was reckless." He was still scowling. "And you don't have a permit."

"What?" Nash and I asked at the same time.

Volkov pointed at the bar. "Molotov cocktails are classified as incendiary devices. You need a federal explosives license to use one. The last thing I need to deal with is the ATF."

I laughed. "You think someone in that bar is calling the ATF?"

A muscle worked in Volkov's jaw as he surveyed the crowd, but he couldn't argue my point.

Nash ran his tongue across his split lip. "Where'd you learn that trick?"

I grinned. "There's an online video for everything."

Volkov shoved a finger in Nash's face before he could respond. "Do not encourage her."

Nash pushed Volkov's finger aside and headed for his truck. "At least this job isn't going to be boring," he called over his shoulder.

Volkov growled but didn't go after him. "Come on. I'll take you home." He wrapped a hand around my upper arm and marched me past the wary bikers to his car. I resisted the urge to give them a finger wave. Barely.

Since I wasn't in the mood for a lecture about my destructive tendencies, I steered the topic to more productive ground. "Any luck with the coven?" I asked when we were both inside his car.

He grimaced. "They were less than helpful."

"It figures," I said, fiddling with the buttons on my side until I found the one that turned the seat warmer on. "The coven likes to pretend that they have no idea some of their members dabble in blood magic. And you are the head of the Tribunal."

Volkov shot me an amused glance as I settled into my now toasty seat with a happy little sigh. He'd probably never sat on a frigid vinyl seat in his life, so he took such luxuries for granted. Not me. I freaking loved these heated seats.

I told him what I found out tonight, including the witch connection. He didn't even gloat.

"So, we're back to sourcing those spell ingredients," Volkov said. "If we find who sold them, there's a good chance they can point us to our witch. If the coven won't answer my questions, I'll go to the Witches' Council and force their hand," he threatened.

The Witches' Council was the world-wide governing body for witches. If they told the local coven to cooperate, they'd have no choice. But dealing with governing bodies was tedious and slow.

"I have a better idea. Pick me up for lunch tomorrow, and then we'll go ask Helen."

Volkov smiled. "It's a date."

"It's not a date," I argued. "It's a working lunch."

His smile widened. "If you say so."

CHAPTER 8

$\mathcal{A}$fter a delicious lunch of smoked brisket, fresh coleslaw, and baked beans, Volkov and I drove to see my witches to source spell ingredients. When we got to the Stitch Witch, the fabric store they owned and operated in Brookside, the place was overrun with eye candy. I watched four muscle-bound men in tiny shorts and tank tops heft the fabric counter off the floor.

Bea crouched down next to them, absentmindedly swishing her mop under the counter while staring. "That's it, boys. Right there."

Other equally hot men carried boxes from the back storeroom and stacked them along the wall. "Not so high," Alyce admonished, smiling as the men squatted to line the boxes single file on the floor instead. With her cherub cheeks and old-fashioned apron, Alyce managed to look wholesome even while ogling men a third her age.

Volkov leaned closer to me. "What the hell is going on?"

I shrugged. With the girls, it was hard to say.

Helen trailed after the men carrying boxes, her eyes lighting up at the sight of me. When she spotted Volkov who now had a hand under my elbow to steer me out of the path of the worker bees, she snapped to attention. "You've got a lot of nerve showing your face here, pup." She poked him in the chest. "After threatening us like you did."

The last run-in these two had, Volkov had threatened to put Helen in a nursing home if she didn't pony up my location. Helen might barely reach his chest, but the woman had made more than one werewolf tuck tail and run.

He glanced at me, and I smiled. He was on his own. At least Volkov had the good sense to look guilty. I wondered if I was about to witness a modern miracle of an alpha apologizing.

"I'd do it again if she were in trouble," he said instead.

Helen gave him the side-eye, but I could tell from her harumph that he'd won her over with that answer. Helen might be a pint-sized terror, but I was her soft spot.

I gestured to the chaos around us. "What's going on?"

"We rented the university rowing team," Bea called, leaning her mop against the wall before making her way over to us.

"You what?" I laughed.

"It's for the children," Helen said with a straight face. "We all have to do our part to support local charities." She snapped her fingers to get the attention of a sandy-haired man with a chiseled jawline and a body you could bounce quarters off. She pointed at the floor. "I think you dropped something there, hon."

I craned my neck for a better view until Volkov reeled me back with a scowl.

Bea watched the two of us. "So," she purred. "You two are finally making it public, huh?"

"It's not like that," I cut in before she could say something outrageous. "We're just working together."

Bea fanned herself. "Workplace romances are hot." She fluffed her dyed blond hair and winked. "Did I ever tell you about my wild fling with the copy machine repairman?"

"No one wants to hear about the two of you making photocopies of your bare asses," Helen interrupted. She spun Bea around and shoved her toward the front of the store. "Go supervise your rowers."

Bea didn't argue, but she did give Volkov an assessing look over her shoulder as she left. "The strait-laced ones always harbor the best kinks," she called.

"Sorry," I whispered when she was out of earshot. "Bea can be a lot."

Volkov caught my gaze and straightened his tie, looking every inch the uptight businessman he could be. He stepped closer and bent his head until his lips brushed the shell of my ear. "She's not wrong."

I bolted for the back room like the coward I was.

Helen barricaded the three of us in the storeroom before facing us with hands on her hips. "Are you in trouble?"

It was a fair question. Now that Carl knew where to find me, it was only a matter of time before he took another run at me. Of course, it would be harder to catch me unaware now that everyone was on the lookout for him and his goons. At least, I hoped so. "No. I'm on a job."

Helen's posture relaxed, and her eyes lit up. "You need a driver?" she asked with a little too much enthusiasm. I'd already promised her the role of getaway driver and witch consultant. She'd refused my offer of a regular cut, insisting I could pay her in potion supplies and a full tank of gas.

"Not yet." I climbed on top of the sturdy storeroom table and tucked my legs underneath me. "We could use your help sourcing some spell ingredients though."

I gestured to the chairs next to me, and both Helen and Volkov sat down. While I filled Helen in on the rogue witch situation, Volkov pulled up his camera roll and handed it to her.

"Here are photographs of the ritual spaces we found," he said, swiping through the first few. "These are from the latest site."

I studied the photos. "Why would the witch leave behind all the spell ingredients?"

Volkov shrugged. "Hard to say. Maybe the witch was interrupted." He turned to Helen. "Do you recognize those ingredients?"

Helen scrolled through the photos, pausing to zoom in and squint at various objects. "Some of these are common spell ingredients like sage and some kind of wood ash." She pointed at the screen. "But that is hemlock." She zoomed in again. "I can't be sure because of the angle, but I think this one looks like datura stramonium, commonly known as Devil's Snare."

"Hemlock is poisonous, so I doubt that's good," Volkov said, looking to Helen for confirmation.

"Probably not," Helen conceded.

"What's Devil's Snare used for?" I asked.

"It's often used as a hallucinogenic. Handled properly, in small doses, it can aid divination." Helen frowned. "But in larger doses, it can be deadly. Combined with the right ingredients and a powerful enough witch, it can be used for coercion or memory manipulation."

"Sounds a lot like the artifact we're chasing," I said.

Volkov nodded. "How easy is it to get these ingredients?"

Helen pointed to a small crystal in the photo. It appeared black but glinted ruby red where the light caught. "This is a blood-fire tourmaline crystal." She whistled. "Incredibly rare. It would be the most difficult to obtain. It'd cost you a pretty penny—or worse, an ill-advised favor."

"What's it used for?" I asked.

Helen continued studying the photo. "Clearing and storing volatile energy, mostly. It can be used to store visions or memories, but that requires a very specialized skill set to pull off."

"What about the hemlock and Devil's Snare?" Volkov asked. "How hard would it be to source those?"

"Officially, all dangerous spell and potion ingredients are controlled, requiring permission from the Witch's Council to obtain," Helen said.

"Unofficially?" Volkov prompted.

Helen handed him his phone back. "If you know what to look for, you can find almost anything at the magical market."

"And I'm presuming you know exactly what to look for," he said, not asking how to find the market itself. As alpha, he probably knew that much.

Helen huffed. "Of course."

Volkov tucked his phone in his jacket pocket. "Good. You can show us."

I unfolded my legs and climbed off the table, eyeing him. "You know you can't go, right?" He stiffened, but I cut him off before he could argue. "You're the poster boy for the authorities. One look at you and every witch selling contraband in the market will clear out."

He clenched his jaw. "It's too dangerous for you to wander around asking questions on your own."

"Good thing I won't be alone then, isn't it?" I patted his bicep and grabbed the station wagon keys from the hook by the door. I tossed them to Helen. "I'll be with the toughest witch in the city."

CHAPTER 9

Despite ditching him back at the Stitch Witch, Max Volkov was lying in wait for us at the arched entrance an hour later when we arrived at City Market. If I hadn't talked Helen into stopping for ice cream, we would have beat Volkov here since he'd obviously taken the time for a change of clothes. Volkov had ditched the suit for a pair of jeans and a faded gray dad sweatshirt—like that would be enough to make him blend in. But instead of making him look like an average dude, he now looked like the kind of man who could kill you with his bare hands and then grill up a perfect backyard steak.

Helen nudged me in the side. "If Bea was here, you know she'd be calling that man daddy right now."

I snickered, imagining the horrified look on his face.

Volkov pushed off the wall he'd been leaning against and stepped into our path. I gave him a slow once over and a wolf whistle. "Someone's been shopping in the lost-and-found."

He ignored me and scanned the area.

City Market took up a full city block. It was laid out with

interconnected vendors and restaurants on all four sides surrounding an open-air courtyard that hosted the weekend farmer's market during warmer months. Each side had an interior walkway with glass garage doors that were rolled up in warmer weather to allow walk-up access to the shops inside. Because it was an unseasonably cold September, the doors were all closed today, and the outdoor farmer's market offerings were sparse.

For those who knew how to spot them, the market provided cover for the vendors who peddled magical items alongside more mundane offerings. The supernaturals who did business here all displayed a spiral symbol somewhere within their business or stall, differentiating them from regular vendors.

Although it had been a long time since I'd shopped the magical vendors as a teenager accompanying Helen, I remembered the protocol. To access the magical inventory, shoppers wore a matching spiral symbol as an iron pendant. Helen pulled hers from beneath her shirt before thumping Volkov on the chest. "If you want intel, we can't be seen with you in there." She pointed to the bustling weekend market.

Volkov brushed Helen's finger aside. "I'm well aware, Helen." He dug his cell phone out of his back pocket, pulled up the photos he'd shown us earlier, and turned to Helen. "Your number?"

She rattled off her cell number, and he sent her the photos.

I raised a brow. "You could have sent them to me instead of driving all the way over here."

Instead of answering me, he scanned the crowd. "I'll hang back on the perimeter, but I've got shifters stationed throughout the market. If you run into any trouble, I'll be there to get you out of it." He shot me a pointed look.

I wasn't sure what kind of trouble he expected to be lurking between tables of butternut squash and bulk spices, but it wasn't worth arguing over. "Fine," I agreed. "But stay out of sight and let us ask the questions. The sooner we find this witch, the sooner I get paid."

He nodded curtly and stepped aside to let us pass.

We stopped at one of the few outdoor produce stalls first. It was located on the west-side, close to the building, and was decorated with intricately carved gourds suspended from the awning, the largest of which bore a spiral design. Although the tables held an ordinary assortment of herbs and late season produce, the woman working the booth noticed Helen's necklace and handed her a specialty item price list.

Helen waited until we were the only shoppers to ask about the hemlock and Devil's Snare. While the two women bent their heads over Helen's phone, I positioned myself in the aisle and blocked as much of the stall as I could while redirecting anyone who slowed down to another vendor.

"Any luck?" I asked as we headed toward the indoor shops a few minutes later.

"More than a dozen purchases of each over the last month." Helen said. "Far too many to narrow it down, especially since only a couple of the buyers were regulars."

When we reached the building, I held the door for Helen. Inside was buzzing with activity. The indoor market held an eclectic mix of shops, with produce and spice bins lining both sides of the walkway. Small clusters of tables sat next to the glass garage doors, providing a view of the courtyard.

I loved the bustle of City Market, with its collective of sights, sounds, and smells. As we stepped inside, bird song drifted down from the rafters where sparrows perched, and shoppers conversed in several languages around us. When I first moved to Kansas City as a teen, I'd sometimes come here to alleviate my homesickness. I'd order a tamarind tea and sit for hours at an empty table. I'd close my eyes and pretend I was home as I listened to the deep baritone of the men speaking Spanish at a table next to me. Although the only Spanish I knew were the curse words I'd picked up from my dad, I didn't need to understand what they were saying to find comfort in their words.

As if she knew what I'd been thinking, Helen gave my arm a squeeze. "You ready, hon?"

I nodded. "Where to next?"

"Sourcing that crystal is our best chance of identifying the buyer, and there's a jewelry store that specializes in magical jewelry and crystals," Helen said.

As we made our way to the other end where the jewelry store was located, the tantalizing smells from the walk-up restaurants made my stomach growl. This part of the market boasted every flavor of deliciousness a girl could want. Unlike the typical suburban mall food court, there wasn't a restaurant chain in sight. From my vantage point, I could see everything from Brazilian food to a hole-in-the-wall Vietnamese place.

"Do we have time for a detour?" I asked, eyeing the Indian food menu taped to the wall next to us.

Helen shook her head. "How can you be hungry? You just ate ice cream."

"Only a small one," I objected. I didn't mention the barbecue.

"Fine but make it quick. Get me a chicken tikka wrap." Helen handed me a ten-dollar bill. "Make it spicy."

She didn't have to tell me twice.

Ten minutes and a full belly later, we stood outside the

jewelry store. I couldn't step foot in a place like this without a lump in my throat and the memory of my mother toiling over her latest creation. More than a decade since I lost her, and I could still recall the smell of a soldering iron when I thought of her. I twisted my mother's ring on my finger—a parting gift I'd claimed from Carl's shop when I ran—and took a steadying breath before stepping inside.

The young woman behind the counter looked like a typical jewelry store employee, all understated elegance in her black-on-black outfit and chic bob. Unlike the delicate silver and gold in the glass display cases, her only jewelry was a heavy spiral pendant identical to the one Helen wore.

"Trixie," Helen greeted the younger woman.

It didn't surprise me that the two women knew each other. As one of the strongest and oldest witches in Kansas City, Helen knew most supernaturals despite operating outside the coven's reach. Although she'd briefly been part of the local coven, her stint had been short-lived. In the seventies, the coven had grudgingly opened their membership to people of color. After Helen joined, it had only taken a few months of watching how the powers-that-be treated Alyce for Helen to leave, taking the most rebellious young witches with her.

Helen, Alyce, Bea, and Janis had been a force to be reckoned with ever since. Even though the Kansas City coven had been inclusive for decades and had tried to coax the women back, Helen had a long memory and a low tolerance for being told what to do. It was one of many things we had in common.

The woman behind the jewelry counter pursed her lips. "I go by Beatrix now."

"Of course." Helen shot her an amused look. "How's your grandma? Still cheating at poker?"

A smile cracked Beatrix's carefully curated exterior. "Like a shark. It's good to see you, Helen."

Since we were the only ones in the store, Helen didn't bother lowering her voice. "We're looking for a rare crystal someone sold recently."

Beatrix's smile dimmed. "All sales are confidential. You know that Helen."

Helen leaned in. "You've heard about the blood magic sites." She hadn't phrased it as a question. News like that traveled fast, and Volkov hadn't tried to keep it quiet.

Beatrix swallowed and nodded. "This is related?"

"It is."

Beatrix looked around, ensuring we were still alone. "I can't give you any names, but if I recognize the crystal, I'll give you as much information as I can." Whether she'd taken a magical oath to guard client confidentiality, or she just didn't want a target on her back from whoever bought that crystal, the tension in her shoulders told us that offer would be the best we'd get.

Helen nodded and pulled out her phone.

Beatrix looked at the photo. She sucked in a breath when she spotted the crystal "Blood-fire tourmaline? You weren't kidding when you said rare." She straightened. "I'm sorry though. We haven't sold anything like it as long as I've worked here."

"How long have you worked here?" I asked.

"Three years."

"Well shit," Helen said. "If you didn't sell it, I have no idea where it came from."

Beatrix bit her lip and looked around to make sure there were no customers lurking over our shoulders. She motioned us closer. "I might have an idea. There's a new place that just opened a few months ago. I haven't been in there myself because the owner gives me the creeps." She wrinkled her nose. "But rumor has it that he deals in rare and dangerous magic."

"Where is this place?" Helen asked.

"You'll find the entrance by the tea cart." Beatrix grabbed Helen's hand before she could leave. "Don't tell him I sent you. I don't want any trouble."

Helen nodded solemnly. "You have my word." Helen made Beatrix promise she'd say hello to her grandmother before we went in search of the tea cart.

CHAPTER 10

e stopped next to the rows of loose tea in glass canisters lining one side of the market walkway. I scanned the area looking for the telltale spiral. Sure enough, the scoops used to portion out the tea leaves had a spiral design etched into their handles.

Helen canted her head toward a walk-up counter where people were ordering drinks. "There."

It took me a second to spot the door with a faint spiral scratched into the wood just beyond the counter. I waited for a lull in the foot traffic before heading for the door. When Helen didn't immediately follow, I turned around to see where she went. At first, I didn't see her through the throng of people surrounding her. When one of them stepped back, I saw her on the floor. A dad with two small children bent down and helped her to her feet before I made it to her side. My nose twitched from the scent of his cheap cologne and the assorted teas as I thanked him. After the crowd dispersed, I pulled Helen off to the side.

"What happened?" I asked. "Are you okay?

She nodded. "Someone knocked me over." Helen scanned the area. "I didn't see who it was because they were behind me." She brushed the dust off her knees and then pulled her cardigan away from her body to examine a jagged hole in it.

I took a closer look. "That looks like it caught on something sharp." I examined her skin, but nothing seemed to be broken. When I searched the area for something sharp, I didn't find anything that would rip a sweater like that.

Helen lifted the cardigan to her nose and sniffed. "Smells like magic."

"Magic?"

"Yeah, but I can't quite place it." Helen shook her head. "I must have caught it on something earlier. It doesn't matter. Let's go see about that crystal." She knocked three times on the door, pausing between each.

"Is that a secret knock?" I asked.

Helen snorted. "No. I don't want to smack someone in the face with the door." When no one answered, she turned the knob and walked inside.

"Smart." I followed her in.

Compared to the bustle and noise of the market, the space beyond the door was unnaturally quiet. While the door was made of heavy wood, I was surprised it blocked as much sound as it did when we closed it, and I wondered if there was an active sound-dampening spell. No one greeted us. A spiral wrought-iron staircase stood in the middle of the empty room.

"I guess we go up," I said.

Something about this place left me unsettled. Maybe it was the echo of Beatrix's warning that whoever owned this shop dabbled in rare and dangerous magic. Whatever it was, I didn't want Helen barreling into trouble. I took the lead.

As I got my first look at the second floor, I stopped at the top of the staircase. The room was a weird mash-up of haunted thrift store and boho trendy. Despite the angled skylights on one side and a bank of windows on the opposite wall, the cloudy day left the room dimly lit. Helen poked me in the back, spurring me into motion again. We stood side-by-side to take it all in.

A cozy seating area in the middle of the room was filled with plush velvet sofas and cheery floor cushions. Half of the far wall was stacked with floor-to-ceiling shoe boxes that looked like they hadn't been opened since the 1950s.

Next to the stacks of boxes were shelves packed full of weird objects. There were collections of rune stones and tarot decks, a couple orbs, several ornate metal and glass containers, and an old-fashioned pendulum. I didn't spot any crystals.

There were, however, row upon row of freaky porcelain dolls with faded paint and dusty dresses. Several of the dolls wore grotesque expressions with milk-white eyes. I shuddered. This was nightmare material if I ever saw it.

I scanned the room. The wall facing the courtyard was made up of a bank of windows covered with macrame plant holders dangling at various lengths. The plants they held were far from ordinary though. I didn't spot a common succulent or spider plant among them. I did see several Venus flytraps and some belladonna, along with a bunch of other plants I didn't recognize.

Helen spotted the wall of plants and inhaled sharply. "Dead man's fingers." Seeing my confusion, she explained. "It's a type of hemlock. Deadly with a twist. It'll kill you but leave you with a joker's smile on your face."

"Very good." The man's voice startled us. "You know your plants."

I spun to face him. He was standing by a daybed and an antique dresser. *Did he sleep here?*

The man was dressed in an old-fashioned tweed vest and tailored pants, with a beard and an honest-to-God gray handlebar mustache. He cradled a wire cage against his chest that held a very pissed off rooster.

I bent my head closer to Helen. "What is this place?"

The man answered. "Whatever you need it to be."

"That's not cryptic at all," I muttered, a shiver of unease chasing down my spine.

He smiled and gestured to a hunter green velvet sofa, a flash of gold peeking out from beneath his long-sleeved shirt. *No smart watches for this guy.*

"Please, have a seat." He hung the bird cage on a brass stand and turned back to us. "Can I offer you tea? I have a selection from the tea cart downstairs."

No way was I drinking anything here after seeing the weird décor. "No thank you," I said before Helen could accept his offer. I led with the obvious question. "Why do you have a rooster in a bird cage?"

The man smiled. "He's a rescue."

The rooster in question was alternating between aggressively pecking the bars and crowing with his chest puffed out. I eyed the cage. *Hopefully, that isn't lead paint he's eating.* "He'd probably be more comfortable in the country," I pointed out.

"Oh, I highly doubt that." The man sat on the sofa across from us. "Now then, what brings you to my door?"

Helen didn't seem the least bit freaked out about this place. She was too busy making herself appear harmless. She hunched her shoulders and twisted her hands primly in her lap, a soft smile curving her lips. I'd learned a long time ago that the frailer Helen looked, the more wary you needed to be.

People always underestimated the little old ladies, and she used that to her full advantage when it served her purposes. I coughed to cover my grin and settled in for the show.

Helen made the introductions, keeping it on a first-name basis. "And you are?" she prompted when the man's gaze remained on me.

"You may call me Isaac."

I noted that he didn't say it was his name.

Helen tilted her head, clearly picking up on the phrasing as I had. "Isaac," she said, "We're searching for a rare crystal, and you come highly recommended."

I stifled a snort, thinking of Beatrix's recommendation.

"What type of crystal are you looking for?" He gestured toward the stacked shoe boxes. "I have quite the collection." His eyes didn't leave mine as he spoke.

"Have you seen this crystal?" Helen held out her phone with the photo. "We're looking for a blood-fire tourmaline."

"I would remember seeing something so rare," he hedged.

Helen narrowed her eyes at the non-answer. "Good. Then you can tell me who you sold it to."

Isaac blinked. "I didn't say I sold it."

It occurred to me why this man made me so uneasy. He barely blinked, which was super creepy. I scooted a little closer to Helen while keeping my eye on him.

"You didn't say you hadn't sold it either," Helen pointed out, all pretense of frailty gone.

The rooster crowed, and Isaac shot it a dark look. But he didn't admit to selling the crystal.

"Whatever this was used for," Helen continued, "it involved blood magic. You can either point me to who bought it, or I can tell the Tribunal member investigating that you own the crystal." She smiled sweetly. "Your choice."

The threat was enough to loosen his tongue. His whole body deflated. "I sold it a few weeks ago, but I can't tell you who bought it."

"Can't or won't?" I asked.

He twirled the end of his mustache and frowned. "Can't. Every time I think of it, my head feels as if it's being split in two."

Helen sat up straighter. "Compulsion?"

"Maybe." He shrugged. "Or a spell."

That certainly fit with the array of ingredients left at the ritual site.

"Altering memories is not a beginner spell," Helen mused. "Even if it is a spell, without knowing who blocked your memory, it's almost impossible to clear."

"There is one way," Isaac said. "But it requires bloodletting."

Helen stiffened beside me. "That's dabbling in darker magic." The rooster punctuated her point with a crow.

"How badly do you want to know who bought that crystal?" Isaac challenged. He glanced at me as if weighing my reaction.

I didn't know enough about spells to make that call. I trusted Helen.

Her face was pinched but after a second, she nodded. "We need to know who has it."

"And you're strong enough to perform such a spell?" he asked Helen.

"Of course."

Isaac stood and walked to a bookcase full of dusty old tomes. "There's an old spell book around here somewhere." He pulled out several before finding what he was looking for. "Ah, here it is. Now, I just need to gather a few supplies."

My stomach pitched as it occurred to me the kind of supplies that might be needed for a bloodletting spell. I scrambled out of my seat and pointed at Isaac. "You better not be talking about harming that rooster."

Isaac held up his hands. "Don't be ridiculous. To access my memories, it has to be my blood."

I sat back down. "That I can live with."

CHAPTER 11

$\mathcal{I}$ expected my first foray into blood magic to be more dramatic. Helen, Isaac, and I were all bent over a scrying bowl watching as a trickle of his blood hit the water. Although he'd used a dagger to cut his finger, I'd had paper cuts that went deeper. All in all, it seemed anticlimactic even with Helen chanting from the tattered grimoire he'd handed her. I gave Isaac the side eye and wondered if he knew what he was doing.

He dipped his finger beneath the surface of the water and gave it a swirl until he was satisfied there was enough blood. Then he pulled his hand out and reached for mine.

I guess this is a holding hands kind of ritual. Reluctantly, I offered him my left hand. Before I knew what he planned, he'd sliced a thin line across my palm with the dagger and clasped my hand in his, making sure to trail his bloody finger across the cut.

"Hey!" I tried to snatch my hand back, but his grip was surprisingly strong for an old guy.

"Blood to blood," he whispered creepily.

I balled my other hand into a fist and drew my arm back to punch him in the balls, but Helen stopped me, holding up the grimoire. "He's right. According to this, you need to be blood to blood to see the memory." She glared at Isaac. "You should have cut my palm though. Riley isn't a witch."

"Even a nonwitch will be able to see the memory. Besides, she's young and healthy, and I didn't want to risk harming you," he reasoned.

If anyone was going to get their palm sliced, I'd rather it be me. "You better not give me hepatitis," I grumbled. I wasn't sure if my shifter genes could heal that or not, and I'd rather not find out.

I nodded for Helen to continue.

"Both of you need to concentrate on the scrying bowl," she instructed before going back to her incantation.

It wasn't until she finished that I felt it. At first, my hand warmed where it pressed against Isaac's, then came the feeling of something crawling under my skin and taking root inside me. It spread like a fever, first in my limbs and then seeping beneath my rib cage before finally settling in my head.

Isaac jerked beside me, but he didn't release his hold. I could sense him inside my head, and it felt wrong. "Something's here," Isaac muttered. "I can feel it."

My heart beat erratically in my chest, and I broke out in a cold sweat. I tried to pull my hand free, but he held firm. It felt like fingers probing, digging around inside my brain. I squeezed Isaac's hand in warning. "I don't like this."

I gritted my teeth against the intrusion. And then it was gone.

As soon as the pain stopped, I saw the memory reflected in the scrying bowl. I concentrated as the picture solidified. It was a woman standing with her back to me. Her auburn hair hit just below her shoulders. She was bundled up in a long black cloak that was belted at the waist, showing off curvy hips and a small waist. I couldn't tell how tall she was since it was hard to gauge height in a scrying bowl. I held my breath as she turned around, ready to catalog every detail so that I could describe her to Helen.

But when the woman faced me, only her eyes were visible. At least they were distinctive, a vibrant green against the gilded mask that covered most of her face. It wasn't some feathered masquerade mask she wore. It was pure gold with elaborate swirls and markings etched into its surface.

This time when I jerked my hand, Isaac let go. With the connection broken, the memory disappeared. I staggered back, putting some distance between us.

Helen's face pinched with concern. "What is it?"

I recounted the memory in as much detail as I could. Helen's brow furrowed when I described the mask. "Pretty eyes and a gold mask aren't a lot to go on," I said.

"I'll ask around," Helen offered. "This witch seems to have a flair for the dramatic, and that tends to get noticed."

It was a long shot. I turned back to Isaac. "Did you recognize her?"

He shook his head. "No. I'm sorry."

"I don't suppose this mystery woman left anything behind?" I asked. A forgotten scarf might retain enough scent that Volkov could identify her.

"Nothing." Isaac kept staring at me like I was a puzzle to be solved.

"Why are you looking at me like that?" When he continued to stare, I shifted uncomfortably. "And what did you mean when you said something was here?"

He stared into the scrying bowl. "When we were connected, I could feel a block of some kind in your mind."

"What kind of block?" Helen asked, setting the grimoire aside.

"I don't know. A memory perhaps." Isaac looked away. "All I could sense was the block itself."

My gut said he was holding something back. Before I could question him further, the door downstairs crashed open and heavy footsteps pounded up the stairs.

"What's the meaning of this?" Isaac demanded as Volkov stormed into the room. Isaac picked up the grimoire and shielded it behind his back as if this were a robbery. Volkov didn't spare him or the book a glance. His gaze immediately found mine. Wisely, Isaac stayed out of Volkov's way when he prowled toward me.

"We have to go. Now." Volkov snapped his fingers at me.

I had too many questions for Isaac to leave now. "I'm in the middle of something."

Volkov growled. "Too bad. Move." He pointed to the stairs.

"Why? What's going on?" Helen asked.

"It's not safe here."

Since he hadn't spared Isaac more than a cursory glance, he couldn't be the danger. Of course, Volkov didn't volunteer any details. He was in full bossy alpha mode. The man was far too accustomed to people doing what he wanted without question. A little explanation would be nice instead of barked commands. When he went for my arm, I scooted out of reach.

Volkov gritted his teeth. "We don't have time for this, Riley." He telegraphed what he was going to do before he lunged for me.

"I'd rethink that move if I were you," I warned.

Volkov ignored me, ducking low enough to grab the back of my thighs as he tossed me over his broad shoulder. *Oh, hell no.* The only place I wanted to be manhandled was in the bedroom.

Helen rubbed her hands together and cackled. "This should be good."

"Last chance to put me down." I kept my voice calm despite the shoulder digging into my gut. I should have skipped that chicken tikka wrap.

Instead of setting me down, Volkov adjusted me so that he had a firmer hold. He demanded Helen follow us and moved toward the stairs. Helen stayed where she was. Isaac paled and put more distance between him and the hostile werewolf.

"Alright. Don't say I didn't warn you," I said.

Volkov didn't answer, but his muscles tensed like he was bracing for me to pummel his back. *As if.* I slid my right hand under the waistband of his jeans and grabbed a fistful of his boxers, yanking as hard as I could while giving them a good twist.

Helen slapped her thigh, flat out belly laughing now.

Volkov stopped abruptly. He finally dropped me to my feet. "For fuck's sake, Riley," he yelled. "Did you just give me a wedgie?"

"I told you to put me down." I scrambled away from him while he adjusted his underwear. There really was no dignified way to pull underwear out of your butt crack. I crossed my arms over my chest and waited until he finished. "I'm not going anywhere until you tell us what's going on. Partners, remember?"

Volkov's eyes blazed, and he clenched his jaw as he got a handle on his temper.

I waited him out.

"Teagan scented an unfamiliar shifter in the market," Volkov said.

Teagan was a fox shifter. I didn't know her well, but she had quickly climbed the pack ranks after moving here a couple years ago. Although the Tribunal's enforcer, Craig Ward, took point on supernatural investigations, she'd helped with several high-profile cases this year. Because Volkov was head of the local pack and the Tribunal, both answered to him. Assigning Teagan to babysitting duty seemed a waste of her talents though.

Although I immediately thought of Carl's threatening voicemail messages, I didn't want to jump to conclusions. I hadn't mentioned Carl's messages to Volkov yet, since there wasn't much either of us could do about the calls, short of changing my phone number.

It was entirely possible that it was unrelated. I inhaled a slow, calming breath. Rogue shifters did occasionally wander into an alpha's territory. It wasn't smart on their part, but it wasn't unheard of either.

Based on Volkov's reaction now, there was more he hadn't told me. "And?"

"And she tracked the shifter to the tea cart downstairs." Volkov's nostrils flared. "The scent was more concentrated there."

Whoever it was hadn't just been passing through this part of City Market then. What were the chances a rogue shifter was here to stock up on loose leaf teas? I hadn't noticed an unfamiliar shifter's scent when we were there, but the man who had helped Helen to her feet had been wearing so much cologne, it had messed with my nose. And as a witch, Helen couldn't distinguish between human and shifter by smell.

"You think it was connected to Carl?" I asked.

It wouldn't be the first time my old alpha Carl sent one of his Santa Fe wolves to keep tabs on me. I forced the knee-jerk panic down that rose every time I thought of Carl. If Teagan tracked the scent that quickly, the shifter was here to send a message. It was the wolf equivalent of peeing on my house, so I'd know he'd been there. That was exactly the type of mind games Carl would play. On the plus side, Carl needed me alive since I was the only one who knew where I'd stashed his precious Alatyr stone when I'd stolen it as a teenager. Whether it was one of Carl's goons downstairs or a random shifter, it didn't change what I needed to do. I had to get that information to Damien Creed ASAP, so he could take out Carl before he got to me.

"I don't know if it's one of Carl's wolves," Volkov admitted. "But we're not taking any chances. I need to get you both out of here."

"Okay," I agreed. Even though I knew I was safe here, surrounded by Volkov and the contingent of shifters he'd brought with him, I also knew that everyone's agitation was going to grow the longer we stayed here. I'd probably gotten as much information from Isaac as I was going to get, anyway.

We were almost to the stairs when the rooster crowed. This time, it sounded more mournful than angry. Isaac rattled his cage until he quieted.

Before I could talk myself out of it, I grabbed the birdcage from the hook and faced Isaac, daring him to argue. "I'm taking the rooster."

"He's a nasty piece of work," Isaac said. "You're welcome to him."

"Don't listen to him." I bent my head, so the rooster and I were eye-to-eye. "Who's a pretty boy?" I cooed.

The rooster preened, fluffing his feathers and tilting his little head as he peered up at me.

"That's right. You're the pretty boy."

Volkov lost the last of his patience and snatched the cage from my hands with a growl. He held it high enough I couldn't wrestle it back and nudged me toward the stairs with his free hand. "You'll get your damn rooster back when we're out of here. Now move."

Helen straightened her spine, shot me a thumbs up, and followed us out the door. Isaac didn't bother seeing us out.

CHAPTER 12

If Volkov insisted on playing chauffeur, I wasn't going to complain. Helen had a shop to run, and taking a rooster on the bus was probably frowned upon. Besides, Volkov's Audi had comfy seats and enough room in the back for the giant birdcage, and despite his animosity toward Nash, he'd agreed to drive me to Stull to check on him. Although Nash had looked fine after the bar fight, some injuries were harder to see than others.

Volkov adjusted his mirror and glared at the rooster as he pulled into traffic. "I'll need directions to Mitchell's place." I didn't miss the tightening of his jaw every time Nash's name passed his lips.

As we walked to his car, I decided I had to tell Volkov about Carl's threatening voicemails in case they were related to the shifter in the market. Although I debated telling him about the deposit Dez had uncovered and our plan to tip off Creed, I kept that part to myself for now. If he knew, Volkov would insist on handling it himself, and after his last run-in with Creed, the last thing he needed to do was tangle with him again.

I'd also filled him in about our visit with Isaac. I described what little I'd discovered about our witch. To avoid the inevitable lecture, I glossed over the blood magic spell we'd performed.

"What type of artifact do you think we're looking for?" I asked in an attempt to make small talk.

Volkov shrugged. "Hard to say."

He merged onto the road, cutting off a jacked-up truck. Had I not spent years riding shotgun with Helen, his aggressive driving might have made me nervous. But it wasn't his driving that had me fidgeting in my seat. I glanced at the dash clock. With weekend traffic, we'd be trapped together for at least fifteen minutes, and we'd already cycled through all the safe conversation topics.

Volkov glanced at my lap where I was tapping my fingers against my leg. "Until we know who was slinking around the market, you should stay at my place."

"Absolutely not."

"Why are you always so difficult?" he grumbled. "You'd be safer at my house."

"I'm not going to pop over for a slumber party every time there's danger," I scoffed, bouncing my right foot before I caught him watching and stilled. "I'm perfectly fine sleeping at my apartment."

"It's not the idea of sleeping that has you twitching like a rabbit about to bolt." He shot me a loaded look. "Let's get this conversation out of the way."

I straightened in my seat. He was right. We'd been dancing around it too long as it was. The sooner we cleared the air, the sooner things could go back to normal. "We're both adults, and we need to be able to work together to find this witch."

"Agreed," he said.

I relaxed, glad we were on the same page. "Just because we slept together doesn't mean things have to be awkward."

"You're right. It doesn't have to be awkward."

This was going better than I expected. "It was a onetime thing."

Volkov smiled. "We both know that's not true."

I stared at him, but his smile didn't falter.

Unwilling to continue that argument, I pulled out my cell phone and texted Dez with an update and the go ahead to send the bank records to Creed. Dez said he'd encrypt the file and have it in Creed's inbox within the hour. I felt the tension drain from my body at Dez's reassurance. Carl wouldn't be my problem for long, and I could go back to concentrating on the job that was going to make me rich.

When we arrived at Nash's place, Volkov refused to wait in the car and didn't offer to carry my birdcage. I wrestled it out of the backseat and set it on the driveway.

"Do you have a napkin?"

Volkov narrowed his eyes. "For what?"

With that cage design, it should've contained the mess. Yet, there was a bright white blob of chicken poop smack dab in the center of his expensive leather seat. I blocked Volkov's view when he tried to peer around me and held out my hand. With a grimace, he handed over a pristine white linen hand-kerchief, ironed into a neat square. I quickly scooped up the mess and rehomed it to Nash's flowerbed.

When I tried to hand Volkov his handkerchief back, he scowled. "Keep it."

I rolled it into a ball and stuffed it into my jean's pocket.

Then I grabbed the birdcage and raced ahead of Volkov to the front door. It was bad enough he insisted on coming inside. If he reached the door first, Nash was likely to slam it in our faces.

After yesterday's excitement, I'd expected to find Nash bright-eyed and ready to take on the world. Instead, Nash answered the door looking like he'd just rolled out of bed after a night of hard drinking. His dirty blond hair and scruffy beard were even wilder than usual, his eyes were bloodshot, and he was shirtless, a Glock tucked in the waistband of his jeans. Everything about him screamed self-destructive. It was a good thing I had the perfect project to distract him.

I pointed to the gun. "I hope that's not loaded."

Nash met Volkov's gaze over my shoulder. "It's always loaded."

"It'll be a real shame when you shoot yourself in the dick, then." I planted a hand on his chest and pushed.

Nash's lips quirked in what could almost pass as a smile before he stepped aside, allowing us in. He was too busy glaring at Volkov to give the massive birdcage I carried more than a cursory glance.

"Nice place." Volkov sneered, taking in the ramshackle museum Nash called home.

I nudged him. "Be nice."

What used to be a modest old house had been transformed into the kind of weird little museum you only found in a small town. The living room we stood in was cluttered with old military paraphernalia. A single army cot against the wall served as Nash's makeshift bedroom. It was a far cry from Max Volkov's upscale home with its high-end finishes and meticulous organization. Volkov was a man who liked everything in its place. The disorder in this room must be making him twitchy.

The only thing well maintained in Nash's space was the guitar leaning against the wall. I'd never heard Nash play, but from the well-loved appearance, I was sure he found as much comfort in music as I did. Maybe I'd invite him to our next karaoke night.

Nash grabbed a shirt from a pile on the floor and put it on, setting the Glock on a table behind him. "I wasn't expecting company."

Volkov scanned for exits before putting his back to the wall and his eyes on Nash. "You probably don't get any."

Nash didn't acknowledge him. "You find the artifact?" he asked me, scowling as he finally noticed the rooster watching him intently from behind the bars of the birdcage.

"No. Not yet, but we're working on it." I bent my head and cooed at the rooster, who was being an angel after shitting in Volkov's car. "He likes you," I told Nash.

Nash grunted, but the fact that he'd asked about the artifact cheered me up. He was coming around.

"Does this mean that you're excited to go after it?" I asked Nash.

He held up a finger to temper my enthusiasm. "One job. That's what I agreed to." He looked at Volkov when he said it. Even though he'd probably agreed to this job more to annoy Volkov than out of excitement to join my crew, I'd take it. He was ex-special forces. Now that he had experienced a taste of that adrenaline rush, he'd be all in. All I needed to do was keep him from crashing.

I held up a hand for a high five, but Nash ignored it. He'd warm up to me, eventually.

"If you haven't located the artifact, then why are you here?" he asked.

I grinned. "I brought you a surprise."

Nash groaned. "It better not be that fucking rooster."

I punched him in the arm. "Stop it. You'll hurt his feelings."

Nash didn't dodge the punch, but he did back away from the cage. "You've got to be shitting me."

"I've been doing some research on the trouble soldiers often have reassimilating into civilian life." Thanks to the Enclave-funded hotspot on my new cell phone, I'd found a lot of interesting information on the subject on the drive here. Both men were now watching me with furrowed brows. "Did you know that having a pet can help with PTSD?" I asked.

Nash stared at me. "Yeah. A dog. Preferably a big dog, like a German Shepherd." His voice rose with every word. "There's no such thing as an emotional support rooster."

I pointed to the rooster. "Meet Garth." Between the acoustic guitar against the wall and his nickname, I figured Nash would appreciate a pet named after a country music legend.

Volkov choked back a laugh. Nash sent him a nasty look that did nothing to quell his amusement.

Nash picked up the cage and shoved it in my arms. "No." Garth squawked at the rough handling and puffed up his little chest.

I tried to soothe him by stroking his feathers through the bars. "Come on. He'll be great for you."

Plus, my apartment might be a hovel, but the landlord wasn't going to let me keep a chicken. My lease didn't allow for pets bigger than a gerbil. The first time Garth crowed, we'd both be out on our asses. On the drive over, I'd Googled how to keep a rooster quiet, and while I found a store that sold anti-crow collars, it seemed cruel to put one on him.

Garth had been through enough. He deserved a better life. Nash had a big yard in a town so small I doubted it had any anti-chicken ordinances. It was perfect.

Volkov's phone rang, startling Garth into crowing again. Although Volkov seemed reluctant to leave and miss the drama, he pulled out his phone. "I'll be back." He took the call outside where he could have a conversation without a rooster crowing in the background.

Nash pointed a finger. "I am not keeping that rooster."

"Garth," I reminded him. Before Nash could object, I opened the cage door, and Garth half flew, half plummeted to the floor at his feet in a mass of ruffled feathers and noise.

Nash scrambled out of the way. "Put him back," he demanded.

I shook my head. "You can't keep him in a cage all the time. It's not healthy."

Nash gritted his teeth. "I'm not keeping him."

"Give him a chance. He needs a home, and I live in an apartment." I squatted down, so I could stroke the little guy's wing. He puffed up but let me pet him. "I rescued him from a witch." I played a bit loose with the facts, hoping to tug on his heartstrings. "He was probably going be the sacrifice in some blood ritual."

"Better that than ending up as nuggets." Nash lunged for the rooster, catching him before Garth could react. He tucked the bird under his arm, effectively pinning his wings. Garth didn't like being manhandled. He pecked furiously at Nash's arm, pulling at least one hair out in the process. "Stop," Nash admonished. Surprisingly, Garth stopped pecking.

"See what a good boy he is?"

The good behavior was short-lived. The second Nash tried to stuff him back into his cage, all hell broke loose. Garth wriggled free and ran, ducking under a nearby table and darting out the other side. Nash gave chase, but the rooster was quicker.

I watched the two of them careening around the room with a smile. This was the most animated I'd seen Nash since he'd tried to kill me. Garth was going to be so good for him.

Nash herded the rooster into the corner of the room before diving for him. Although Nash got a hand on him, Garth wasn't going back in that cage without a fight. Nash came up with a handful of feathers, but Garth took off at a run while flapping his wings. The flight wasn't pretty, but he managed to get airborne.

Garth landed on top of a musket mounted on the wall. From there, he launched himself again, making it all the way to the wood beam that spanned the length of the room. Like a lot of older houses, this one had ten-foot-high ceilings. In order to mount a ceiling fan low enough to be useful, the beam was several feet below the ceiling. Based on Garth's happy crows, it made an ideal perch.

Nash shook his fist at the bird and yelled, but Garth stayed where he was. When Nash started swearing, Garth cocked his head to the side, wiggled his fluffy butt, and dropped a load that narrowly missed Nash's upturned face.

Volkov picked that moment to come back into the room. "We need to go. We've got a lead on Isaac's witch."

Nash glared at me. "Don't even think about leaving him here."

I peered up at the beam and shrugged. "Even if I wanted to take him with me, I can't reach him." I patted Nash on the shoulder. "Don't worry. You've got this. I'll be back to check on him soon. I'll even pick up some chicken feed and treats. Give him scraps until then, and you'll win him over in no time."

I didn't allow myself to linger. A clean break was best for everyone.

CHAPTER 13

Gwendolyn Reynolds was a thirty-three-year-old witch with a green thumb and a talent for potions. According to Helen, Gwen mostly kept to herself since moving to Kansas City several months ago. She worked in a local greenhouse and lived in a row of townhouses off a busy street in a run-down part of town. It wasn't hard to spot her place. The small patio entrance was overrun with potted plants and trellised flowering vines.

Since Gwen hadn't been home when we made it back to Kansas City last night, Volkov had pack members watching her place until we could intercept her after work today. Two of his shifters were now covering the rear of the building in case Gwen saw us and decided to slink out the back.

"Let me take the lead," Volkov said as we got out of his car.

He'd almost worded it as a request. Definite progress. I nodded and followed him across the townhouse parking lot.

A car pulled in, and a woman matching Helen's description climbed out. Volkov and I exchanged a glance. Catching her outside would be much easier than coaxing her to the door once she got inside her house. I wasn't above breaking and entering, but if we could do this the easy way, I was all for it. The woman opened the back door of her car and reached inside for a bag of groceries. Volkov positioned himself between her and the townhouse, and I boxed her in from behind.

"Gwen?" Volkov's voice startled her, and she bumped her head on the car frame as she straightened.

She clutched her reusable bag to her chest as she turned to face him. "You scared me."

I stepped to the side, where I was still within arm's reach but not in a position to spook her further. From here, I could see her face. Although she wore glasses, those forest green eyes were a dead ringer for the memory Isaac showed me. This was definitely her.

"Do I know you?" she asked Volkov, no doubt thinking he wasn't a man she'd easily forget meeting.

"Max Volkov," he introduced himself with a smile and an outstretched hand.

He was better at intimidation than putting a skittish witch at ease though. As if she sensed the threat, she took a step away from him before finally noticing me. It didn't take her long to dismiss me and return her attention to Volkov. She lowered her voice. "You're the alpha of the Kansas City pack?"

"I am. I need to ask you a few questions."

She shifted the bag nervously. "What kind of questions?"

"It would be best if you came with us," he said, gesturing toward his car.

Not surprisingly, she didn't leap at the chance to get in a car with two strangers, one of whom was built like an NFL linebacker. Gwen shook her head. "I don't know you. You'll have to ask your questions here."

"Fine," Volkov agreed. "Do you know a witch who goes by the name of Isaac and operates out of a shop in City Market?"

I watched Gwen's reaction closely and noticed the flicker of recognition at Isaac's name. Her gaze darted to her town-house as if gauging the distance and her chances of outrunning a werewolf.

"I wouldn't run from him if I were you," I warned. "This will go much easier if you cooperate."

Naturally, she ignored my warning and threw the bag of groceries at Volkov before sprinting for the safety of her townhouse. Volkov dodged the bag and caught Gwen by the arm with a warning growl.

"Stop." He put the full weight of an alpha's command behind the order, and she froze momentarily. Alpha commands weren't as effective on non-shifters, but they were still difficult to ignore. "Let's try this again." Volkov kept his hold on her arm and marched her toward his car.

I paused long enough to pick up the bell peppers and canned goods on the ground, stuffing them back into her grocery bag and putting it inside her car. Better not to draw attention to our forced chat. I turned in time to see Volkov grab his shoulder, releasing his hold on Gwen. She took advantage, bolting for the street.

"What's wrong?" I shouted, running toward him.

Volkov pivoted, blocking the street with his body as he met me halfway. Now that he was facing me, I could see the ragged hole in his dress shirt and the trail of blood beneath it. "Gun shot," he said, spinning me and shoving me behind a nearby car before crouching down beside me.

As a shifter, a bullet wound to the shoulder would be little more than an inconvenience. With his accelerated healing, he probably wouldn't even have a scar by morning. My heart still raced as I ran my fingers along his collarbone to feel for the wound.

He stilled my hand. "It just grazed me."

The blood on my fingers said otherwise.

He met my eyes. "I'll be fine. Stay here. I'm going after the shooter." He stood and ran in the opposite direction as Gwen, making sure to weave as he went.

Screw that. "I'm going after Gwen!" I kept my body low as I ran.

I was a lot faster on my feet than Gwen, but she had a solid head start and panic driving her. She didn't wait for a break in the cars, darting into ongoing traffic like she had a death wish.

"Stop," I yelled, not wanting her death on my conscience. "I just want to talk."

She didn't slow down, even as she bounced off the fender of a sedan that screeched to a halt as it struck her. The concerned driver hastily put his car in park and got out to make sure she was okay. Instead of taking off again, Gwen waited for him before pointing at me. "That woman attacked me."

By now, we'd drawn a crowd, and all of them were staring straight at me. I knew what they saw. With her long auburn hair and trendy glasses, Gwen looked like a librarian. And I was a pink-haired woman sporting tattoos and an anarchy t-shirt. No one on the planet would see her as the threat, even if I hadn't been chasing after her. And unlike Volkov, I couldn't command them to do anything.

Because I wasn't a match for an angry mob, I paused at the edge of the road as the man hustled her into the backseat of his car and sped away. I stared after them, memorizing the license plate number in hopes Volkov could track the driver down and find out where he took her. Not that it would do us much good. Gwen was probably smart enough to have him drop her off in a public place.

"Damn it." I stood there catching my breath until I felt a hand at my back. I knew who it belonged to by scent alone. "Did you catch the shooter?"

"No." Volkov's voice was strained.

I turned around, paling when I saw a bead of sweat on his forehead and the gray tint to his skin. "What's wrong."

Volkov held up his hand, a bullet between his thumb and forefinger. "Silver."

He swayed on his feet, and I caught him, staggering under the weight.

"Don't you dare die on me," I yelled at Volkov when he stumbled again. I wrapped my arm more securely around his waist and concentrated on keeping us both upright.

"I'm not dying," he said with a laugh. "It'd take a lot more silver than a bullet to kill me."

I dug my fingers into his side. "It's not funny." I blinked away the unexpected tears that blurred my vision.

"Hey." He stopped in the middle of the sidewalk, forcing me to stop with him. "I'm not dying," he repeated. "It's just the effects of the residual silver. I'll be okay. Give me a minute, and I'll be fine to drive."

Even though the bullet went straight through Volkov's shoulder, the trace amount of silver it left behind was definitely affecting his reflexes. "You are not driving." I was yelling again, but I couldn't seem to muster a calm voice. I wondered if this is how he felt every time I had a brush with death. "Give me your keys, and I'll drive."

Volkov made a sound like he was being strangled. For a

second, I was afraid he had an internal injury he hadn't told me about until I caught his horrified expression. "You're never driving my car," he said.

I wasn't that bad of a driver, but now didn't seem like the time to argue. "Fine. I'll call Teagan." I nudged Volkov to get moving again. We made it to the bus stop next to the busy street, where I lowered him to the bench. He sagged against it, the silver making his movements sluggish. I fished his cell phone out of his pocket with shaky hands.

I held his cell phone up. "Unlock it."

He winced as he reached for it with his bad shoulder, but he did as I asked.

Volkov refused to relinquish his keys until Teagan showed up. Teagan raced us to the Stitch Witch. I'd called ahead, so Helen and Alyce were waiting for us at the backdoor. Teagan parked in the alley behind the shop and jumped out to help.

By the time we made it inside, Volkov had regained some of his color. Helen pointed to a chair, and he dropped into it. Alyce probed his wound with the efficiency of an army medic. After applying a poultice to draw out any silver remaining in his body, she bandaged him up with gauze and medical tape.

Alyce patted him on the knee. "All patched up. You'll be as good as new tomorrow," she promised.

Teagan waited until Alyce finished. "What happened?" she asked.

"I had ahold of Gwen, and we were halfway to my car when the bullet hit me. After getting Riley to cover," he paused to glare at me, "where she should have stayed, I went after the shooter." Volkov rolled his shoulder as if to work the stiffness out.

Alyce swatted his good arm. "Be still before you screw up all my hard work."

"Did you get a good look at the shooter?" Teagan cut in.

"No. I picked up his trail though."

I swallowed. "Shifter?"

Volkov nodded. "The same one who was hanging around the market."

"Where did it lead?" Teagan asked.

"I followed it across the street, but—" He frowned. "When I got there, the scent was gone."

That wasn't normal. I didn't have a wolf's nose, but even I didn't lose a scent that fast. "How is that possible?"

Helen and Alyce exchanged a look.

"Well?" I prompted.

"They're not cheap, but a scent-masking spell would do it," Helen said.

Alyce nodded her agreement.

Volkov muttered about meddlesome witches under his breath until Alyce stared pointedly at his bandaged shoulder. He grabbed a scrap of fabric from the nearby worktable and used it to dig the silver bullet out of his pocket. He handed the cloth bundle to Teagan. "I went back for it after I lost the trail."

Teagan examined the bullet with Helen and Alyce peering over her shoulder. "People don't use silver bullets for a random drive-by."

"No," Volkov agreed. "I don't think they were aiming for me though. Gwen was struggling, which is what put me in the line of fire."

"Where would it have hit if you hadn't moved into the path?" Teagan asked.

"My best guess is that it would have gone between Gwen and me." Volkov looked at me. "And you were behind us."

"You think they were shooting at me?" I asked.

He nodded. "I do."

"Maybe the shooter was aiming for the witch," Alyce suggested.

"Not with a silver bullet they weren't," Volkov argued.

I joined the women staring at the bullet like it held the answer.

"Why wouldn't the shooter use the scent-masking spell to begin with?" I asked, the answer coming to me before I finished voicing the question "Unless the shifter wanted us to know he was there. It was a warning."

Helen put her hands on her hips and glared at it. "It had to be Carl. That no good, mangy excuse for an alpha."

Alyce crossed the room and pulled me into a hug, all grandmotherly reassurance. "Don't you worry, honey. I've got enough money set aside to hire a hitman."

Teagan sputtered. She hadn't spent much time around my witches. "There are laws. You can't just have someone killed." She looked to Volkov for backup, but he seemed to like Alyce's approach to dealing with the problem. Teagan threw up her hands. "We have a system for a reason. People are going to ask questions if an alpha turns up dead, you know." She pointed at me. "And Riley here will be the number one suspect."

Helen snorted. "Like we'd be dumb enough to leave the body."

I jumped in before this could devolve into a fully fleshed out murder-for-hire plot. "You keep your moonshine money," I told Alyce. "If that bullet was meant for me, then it rules out Carl."

Everyone stared at me.

"How do you figure?" Teagan asked.

"If that shot had been on Carl's orders, they wouldn't have

wasted the silver. Straight-up lead is a lot cheaper and easier to find." I might heal faster than a human, but a direct hit between the eyes or to the heart would still kill me, regardless of the metal of the bullet.

"Maybe Carl didn't want you dead." Volkov reasoned. "You said it yourself. Until you give up the location of that stone you took from him, you're more useful to him alive. But half delirious from silver-poisoning? It's a great way to loosen your tongue."

"There's one problem with that theory," I said, reaching for the bullet. I didn't bother with the scrap of fabric, closing my hand and pressing the bullet into my palm. "Everyone in Carl's pack knows silver has no effect on me. When I lived with Carl, one of my jobs was polishing the silver and turquoise jewelry we sold out of the pawnshop because I was the only one who could handle it without breaking out in a rash." I opened my fist to show my unblemished hand.

Volkov grabbed my wrist and tugged me closer to examine it. "I've never heard of a shifter immune to silver."

"Neither have I." Teagan angled her body for a better look.

I handed the silver bullet back to Teagan and shrugged. "Goat shifter." Just like my immunity to alpha commands and vampire compulsions, silver had no effect on me. Never had.

Volkov rubbed his thumb across my palm as if double-checking before releasing it.

I held up my left hand. "How did you think I wore this?" I tapped the delicate silver ring on my finger. My mother had designed and crafted it, etching the jewel flower design herself.

"I assumed it wasn't real," Volkov said with a frown.

Teagan interrupted. "So, if it wasn't one of Carl's shifters, then who'd have a reason to shoot you?"

"No one," I insisted. Other than Carl, I didn't have enemies. On the heels of Carl's threatening messages, I'd jumped to the logical conclusion that this shifter was connected to him. But he wasn't the only person with shifters on his payroll and a vendetta to settle.

I spun to face Volkov. "Or maybe the shooter was targeting you after all. Alyce isn't the only one with enough rainy-day funds to hire a professional, you know. When we stole that war scythe, we made a fool out of Damien Creed. And he had your name."

Because Creed ran Volkov's prints, he knew exactly who had crashed his auction. There was no way that he wouldn't have connected the missing war scythe and Volkov's escape the same night. Damien Creed might not be willing to risk the Enclave's wrath by coming after Volkov directly, but that didn't mean he was above sending someone else in to even the score. Hell, with the information Dez uncovered showing that Creed bankrolled Carl's power grab for the Santa Fe alpha position, it might still be one of my old packmates taking the shot, even if I hadn't been the target.

I swallowed, fear coiling in my belly. If this was a hit, there would be another attempt.

"Coming after the head of the Tribunal would be reckless," Teagan argued.

Helen sighed. "Only if the kill could be traced back to Creed."

She made a good point, but Volkov seemed unconvinced.

I'd already jumped to one conclusion when I'd assumed it had been connected to Carl. I didn't want to do it again, so I considered all the possibilities.

"There is another explanation," I said. "Even if the shooter wasn't aiming for the witch, we can't rule out it being related.

We know that Gwen is the witch connected to the ritual sites because she was the one in Isaac's memory. But we have no idea whether that memory was before or after Luca Cardelli acquired Valac's artifact."

"If Gwen was his contact here in Kansas City, he could have double-crossed the Enclave and sold it to her," Volkov finished.

I thought back to Gwen's modest car and generic groceries. She didn't act like someone with enough money to buy a rare artifact. "Or maybe she was fencing it for him?"

"It's possible," Volkov conceded, but he didn't sound convinced. "You think Cardelli might be a shifter?"

"Could be." I really had no idea, and Sato wasn't very forthcoming with details. "If Cardelli double-crossed the Enclave, it would make sense that he wouldn't want Gwen talking to us."

Volkov stood and shoved the bullet back in his pocket. "Instead of sitting around here speculating, I'd rather go get some answers."

"You're right." I grabbed my jacket and Helen's keys. "Can you give me a ride to see Dez? He can check the traffic cams to see if we can ID the shooter." If one of Carl's wolves was on the footage, there was a good chance I'd recognize him. And if it was someone else, we could at least rule out Carl.

"Sure, hon." Helen took the keys and headed out the door.

Volkov followed us out. "Teagan, you're with me. Let's go track down the witch."

CHAPTER 15

The only face I recognized on the traffic cam footage was Gwen's as she slid into the passenger seat of her good Samaritan's car. Dez and I not only watched the traffic cam footage but also reviewed the security footage from the nearby strip mall to no avail. Whether it was a stranger, or the shooter had been smart enough not to be caught on camera, it was a dead end.

"What now?" Dez asked before eating a noodle out of the ramen we were splitting.

I shrugged. "I don't know. Without a scent to follow or a face on camera, our mystery shifter is hard to track. Hopefully, Volkov is having better luck." I dug in the container with my chopsticks and came up with a chunk of meat. It took all my concentration to get it to my mouth.

Dez laughed, watching me. "Why don't you just use a spoon?"

"You can eat with these. I'm going to figure this out, eventually." I fumbled my bite and had to duck my head to catch it before turning my attention back to the matter at hand. I glanced at Dez. There had to be a way to search more thoroughly than combing through security footage. "Hey Dez, can we use facial recognition software to see if any of Carl's men are in Kansas City?"

"I mean, it's possible but inefficient. Coverage is spotty and spread among a lot of disconnected cameras. But I have another idea." He grabbed his computer. "After our last run-in with Carl, I started tracking his credit card usage. If he uses any of his cards within a fifty-mile radius, I get an alert on my phone."

I whistled. "That's handy."

Dez gave me the laptop and pointed to the blank doc he'd pulled up. "Make me a list of every pack member you remember. First and last names. I'll add them to the script and add your cell number to the alerts. We'll get a notification if any of them use a card in this area."

"That's brilliant." I gave him a quick hug. A few weeks ago, he would've stiffened up, but Dez was getting used to me. He squeezed me back without hesitation. I reached out and felt his bicep. "Have you been working out?"

He swatted my hand. "A little."

I hid my surprise. Dez seemed more like the bike-to-work than a weightlifting kind of guy, but I was happy to see him throwing himself into new activities. For a long time after being turned, he'd been in a bad place. "Good for you!"

Dez turned serious. "I figured if I'm going to be part of this team, I need to pull my weight."

I pointed to his computer. "You more than pull your weight with that, Dez."

He shrugged. "Maybe. But I don't want to be a liability in a fight." A fang punched through his gums, and he touched it with his tongue. "Like it or not, I'm a vampire. It's about time I used that to my advantage."

Although I would've loved to argue that he didn't need to change, he already was. "Does this mean you're going to start drinking from the tap?" I joked. Dez had a serious gag reflex when it came to drinking blood.

Dez ran a hand through his messy red hair. "Hell no."

My phone rang, with Volkov's number on the screen. I picked up. "Any luck finding our witch?"

"Oh, I found her alright," Volkov said. "She ran straight to the coven, and they're protecting her. They are refusing me access. Can't let a werewolf into their inner sanctum." He sounded at the end of his patience.

"Maybe they'll let me talk to her," I offered. I was hardly the threat Volkov posed.

"No shifters allowed," he bit out.

I stood up and tossed the empty container into the trash. "Okay, then I'll call Helen. She's a tough interrogator. Trust me. That woman will crack Gwen in no time." I'd been on the receiving end of her questioning more than once as a teen, and she was ruthless. "We'll meet you there in an hour. I need to make a stop first." I hung up before he could ask questions.

With Gwen under the coven's protection, there was no better time to check out her townhouse. I'd be in and out in fifteen minutes and at coven headquarters in time to meet Helen for the interrogation. I called Helen and told her what we needed. At the mention of a showdown with the coven, she was all in. I had no doubt she'd show up with reinforcements.

With his vampire hearing, I didn't have to repeat the conversation for Dez. "You want to go see Helen take on the powers that be?" I asked him.

He grinned. "Hell yeah, I do." He ducked into his kitchen. "I'll grab the popcorn."

I borrowed a hooded sweatshirt from Dez's closet to hide my distinctive hair. I'd already made a spectacle of myself chasing Gwen across the parking lot. I didn't need anyone calling the cops as soon as they spotted me. I also grabbed the yellow latex cleaning gloves Dez kept under his kitchen sink. Then we headed over to Gwen's townhouse to do a little snooping.

Although it took some convincing, Dez eventually agreed to wait in the car while I circled around back. Fortunately, I never left home without my trusty lock-picking kit, which made quick work of the back door. The inside of Gwen's townhouse was covered with even more potted plants than her outdoor patio.

If Gwen had Valac's artifact, I was hoping she kept it close. I might not know exactly what I was searching for, but a demon relic shouldn't be hard to spot among her coordinated Pottery Barn décor. I started in the bedroom, checking beneath the bed before going through her nightstand, dresser, and closet.

I'd broken into enough houses in my youth to learn you could tell a lot about people from the contents of their closets. For example, Gwen's collection of sensible shoes with well-worn soles told me that she was both practical and hard-working. Over half of her closet was dedicated to skirts and classy shirts in understated hues despite the fact that she worked in a greenhouse. Either they were from a previous life as an office drone or Gwen was careful to cultivate an image out of step with her daily life. Fencing that artifact would be a surefire way to upgrade her life.

The most telling item in her closet wasn't an article of

clothing though. It was a dingy stuffed bear that she'd obviously carted around for years. Unlike the carefully curated wardrobe and the tasteful interior decorating, the bear had a patch on his belly, countless stains and dings, and a torn ear. But it wasn't tucked away on a top shelf or shoved into a box of mementos. The tattered stuffed animal sat on a prominent center shelf without a speck of dust on it. Despite all the trappings of her life, this was what she valued.

I made quick work of the rest of the townhouse but came up empty-handed. If Gwen was in possession of the demon artifact, she wasn't keeping it here. After putting everything back the way I found it, I jogged back to Dez's car.

Twenty minutes later, we pulled up to the coven headquarters in time to see Alyce lob a magical smoke bomb through an open window before cupping her hands to give a goggled Helen a boost up to the sill. The other two witches were watching from the sidelines. Janis was nervously twisting her long skirt in her hands while Bea prowled the perimeter shouting at the coven leadership, presumably in an attempt to provide Helen and Alyce a distraction. Volkov was nowhere in sight.

Dez rolled down his windows, shut off the car, and reached for his microwave popcorn before reclining his seat to settle in for the show.

I opened the passenger-side door. "Wish me luck. I'm going in."

He waved me off, still watching the unfolding drama.

Since Janis was the only witch who wasn't involved in the siege, I walked straight to her. "She was supposed to wait for me."

Janis gave me a pitying look. "And you believed her?"

I sighed. She was right. I should've known that Helen

would march straight in and stir up trouble.

"Why did she climb in through the window?" I asked.

"Oh, she's already met with the coven leadership," Janis said.

I cringed. "I take it the negotiations didn't go well?"

Janis snorted. "Those stuck-up hacks told Helen she was no longer welcome on the premises. One of the younger ones even asked if she needed assistance getting back in her car."

I pressed my lips together. That was like waving a red flag in front of a bull. No wonder she was storming the gates. "Looks like she's in," I observed as Helen's white orthopedic sneakers disappeared through the open window.

Knowing Helen, I half-expected her to march Gwen out by the ear, but when she came out ten minutes later, she was alone. "No luck?" I asked.

She curled her lips. "Those cowards barricaded themselves in the potion storeroom. Claimed they called the cops."

As soon as she said it, I made out the faint sound of sirens getting closer. "We should probably go."

Helen crossed her arms over her thin chest. "They're bluffing."

I nudged her toward her station wagon, but she planted her feet. "Maybe. But I'd rather not have to explain to the police why we're demanding access to a woman caught on a traffic camera fleeing as I chased her."

"You're right. You can't be caught here." She pointed to Dez's car. "Go. I'll cover your getaway."

"I'm not leaving you here," I insisted.

Volkov's black Audi pulled up, breaking up our argument. He rolled down his window. He did not look happy. "What happened to meeting here in an hour and going in together?"

I held up my hands. "I just got here."

Volkov shook his head. "We're not getting anywhere near Gwen now. Bennie gave me a heads up. Cops are on their way." Bennie was not only a member of Volkov's pack, he also worked as a dispatcher. He was one of many embedded within human emergency services, which allowed him to route calls involving supernaturals to more appropriate authorities—usually Volkov. A tic formed in Volkov's jaw as he stared at Helen. "The coven claimed Helen here was attempting to break in. Said she was a danger to herself." He leveled Helen with his no-nonsense alpha stare. "You know what that means."

Helen straightened to her full height, which still didn't top five feet, and nodded. "That means they need a demonstration of the kind of danger I can be."

Volkov threw the car in park and opened the door. Without saying a word, he scooped Helen off the ground and carried her to her station wagon before setting her inside. Helen was so stunned that she didn't take a swing until he buckled her seatbelt. He caught her second punch in his palm and leaned in. "Behave. Getting yourself arrested is exactly what the coven wants."

It was probably the only thing he could have said that would actually get Helen to back down. "Fine. We'll regroup at the shop and wait out the heat."

Volkov closed her door and pointed to a nondescript car parked across the street. "My men will make sure the witch doesn't escape in the meantime."

One look at the tension in his shoulders, and I declined Volkov's offer of a lift in favor of riding shotgun with Dez. Before he arrived at the Stitch Witch, Dez and I polished off the last of the popcorn while watching the video he took of Helen going through that window.

Apparently, the coven not only labeled Helen a walking menace, they also reported Volkov to the Witches' Council, claiming he was abusing his power by demanding access to Gwen. It was bullshit, of course, but working through the bureaucratic hurdles would take weeks we didn't have. According to Helen, the coven had also warded all but the entryway to keep out any supernaturals other than coven members. We'd all spent the last thirty minutes brainstorming ways to bypass their security measures.

As a goat shifter, magic didn't always work on me like it did on other people. At least that was true for compulsions and commands. For whatever reason, I seemed to be different enough to other shifters that it created a magical loophole I could use to my advantage. It was possible that a general ward against shifters wouldn't extend to me unless the coven specifically warded against my entry.

I sat cross-legged on top of the worktable. "It's worth the risk," I argued. "I could at least try to get past their wards."

When no one immediately agreed with me, I tried again. "What's the worst that could happen? A magical zap?"

"Absolutely not," Volkov said.

I ignored his knee-jerk denial. "Helen?"

"He's right," Helen said, clutching her chest like it pained her to say so. "These aren't trifling wards meant to warn off intruders, hon. I heard the incantations as they were setting them. The wards are lethal."

Volkov paced the room, growing more agitated with every step. As a Tribunal member, he was used to being able to strong-arm access to anywhere he wanted. If there wasn't so much at stake, I'd enjoy him getting a taste of what the rest of us faced on a daily basis.

Volkov paused his pacing long enough to give Dez a considering look. "If I got you a human cop, could you compel him to arrest Gwen?"

Dez seemed dubious. "I could try."

Helen shot the idea down. "It's too messy. If the witches manage to break the compulsion, it would not only expose us to a human, it would also get Dez arrested."

She had a point. Besides, the last time Dez tried to compel someone, it hadn't gone well. And that gave me another option. "I have a better idea."

Everyone looked at me expectantly, and I smiled.

"What we need is a human who can sneak past the wards—someone with the skill set to infiltrate a hostile environment and retrieve an uncooperative witch for interrogation." I tapped my chin. "Sound like anyone we know?"

Volkov scowled as I scrambled off the table to get my phone, but he didn't deny it.

Dez, on the other hand, spoke up. "I don't know, Riley. Even if you can convince Nash Mitchell to do this, he's not exactly dependable. I don't think we can count on him for this."

I knew Dez wasn't Nash's biggest fan. Taking a punch to the face didn't exactly facilitate bonding. But disliking someone didn't always render them untrustworthy. Since I didn't want to discount Dez's feelings, I chose my words carefully. "Remember that you have access to information that Nash wants. He might say no," I conceded even though I was sure I could convince him, "but I think he wants that intel on the op that ended his career enough to do this."

"I guess that's true," Dez conceded.

"Just give him a chance, Dez. That's all I'm asking," I said. "Think of this job as an extended interview. If by the end of the job, you still think he's the wrong fit, I won't force it."

"Alright. I'll give him a chance," he agreed. Dez still didn't look happy about bringing Nash in on this, but he held any other objections.

It was harder to convince Nash to leave Garth at his house than it was to get him to agree to kidnap a witch. He really wanted to unload that rooster, but I was convinced they just needed time to bond. Besides, at this time of night, Garth was already happily settled on his perch.

After relaying everything I knew about the situation he'd be facing over the phone, Nash instructed me to meet him a block from the site an hour after dark. After checking with Dez, I assured Nash that we could get both the layout of the building and the number and location of the occupants by then.

All we needed was a rendezvous point.

"There's a coffee shop on the corner," Alyce offered. "They make the best raspberry scones."

Volkov shot her a disbelieving look. "We are not planning a snatch and grab over tea and scones."

"Coffee," Alyce corrected.

He stared at her until she huffed in annoyance, mumbling about young bloods being too big for their britches.

Dez had been unusually quiet since I'd suggested bringing Nash in, but he finally perked up. "I've got the perfect solution. I've been saving it as a surprise, but you know that florist van you wrecked?"

"A minor fender bender," I corrected.

"The body shop might disagree," Dez said. "There was enough damage that it was easier to buy it from the owner."

My shoulders slumped. He'd borrowed it for me. Although I'd fully intended to pay for the damage, I'd been so preoccupied with everything else, I hadn't even checked to make sure it had been repaired. "I'll pay you back," I promised.

He waived me off. "We'll bill the Enclave for it and call it an operating expense."

My guilt eased. "Good plan."

"I figured the van would come in handy, so I had the body damage repaired and retrofitted it for surveillance." Dez grinned. "I loaded it up with all the bells and whistles. You want to see?"

I rubbed my hands together. "Do you really need to ask?"

Dez was already halfway to the door. "I left it at the body shop until I could find a place to park it." It was probably a bad idea to keep a van meant to be incognito next to his apartment complex.

"Anyone else up for show and tell?" I asked.

Helen patted my arm. "You two go have fun. We've got a quilting demonstration this afternoon."

I looked at Volkov.

"Pass," he said. "I'll be there when Mitchell shows up."

"Suit yourself." I followed Dez out.

He was practically vibrating with excitement as he told me all about the high-tech gear he'd installed. "Don't worry," he assured me when I protested him spending so much of his own money on our Scooby van. "I've kept itemized records for the equipment reimbursement."

With neither of us on the hook for the cost, I relaxed into my seat. "Add a drone and night vision goggles to the list."

Dez gave me a thumbs up. "Already done."

CHAPTER 17

We parked our new D&R Cleaning Co. van down the block from the coven headquarters. By the time Volkov showed up, Dez had an infrared map of the occupants, a 3D model of the interior, and video feeds showing the main room, the hallways, and the storeroom. Unfortunately, the rec room and the wing of bedrooms that the coven maintained for out-of-town guests were camera free. Even Volkov tossed out a "good work" when Dez gave him the rundown.

While the three of us waited on Nash, we debated the best way to get to Gwen. Not surprisingly, Volkov advocated for the most direct approach. I argued for going in through a rarely used window, and Dez played referee. Despite the discreet cameras mounted above both license plates, I didn't see Nash coming. Volkov was the only one who didn't look surprised when Nash opened the passenger-side door and joined us.

I had wondered how Nash would dress for an op like this. From the dark clothes and quiet footwear to the balaclava around his neck, ex-special forces badasses dressed a lot like burglars. I tipped my chin in approval.

Nash didn't waste time on small talk, directing his question to me. "You got the intel I need?"

I pointed to Dez who sat across from me watching a bank of monitors and surveillance equipment. Dez had stiffened the minute Nash appeared, and he didn't relax when Nash finally acknowledged him. "Dez is our resident tech genius," I said.

Nash scanned the equipment lining the van. "He's got the toys right at least."

Dez bristled when Nash reached around him to flip through the video feeds. "Don't touch my things." He rolled his chair to block Nash. "I'll translate and try to use small words, so you can understand."

My eyes widened, and Volkov barked out a laugh.

Nash studied Dez. "How's the eye, kid?"

The last time these two were in the same room, Nash gave Dez his first black eye. From the red bleeding into Dez's vision, he was considering payback.

I put myself between them before they came to blows. My visions of a cohesive crew were growing tarnished by the minute. "We're on the same team, guys." Hopefully now that the posturing part of the evening was over, they could learn to work together. All they needed was a common goal. I pointed to the monitor behind Dez. "Can you get Nash up to speed?"

Dez ran through everything again, noting the concentration of heat signatures in the rec room where most of the coven members still on site were congregated before pointing to the sole person in the bedroom. "That's our witch." He pulled up Gwen's driver's license photo.

Nash took a good look before leaning toward the second monitor that showed the 3D model of the building.

"The easiest access points—" Volkov started.

Nash held up a hand. "I don't need your input." He turned to me. "Keep your eye on the building and open the back doors the second you spot me."

I nodded. "Got it."

Nash did a quick check of his gear, including his gun.

"Leave the gun," Volkov ordered. "We want to question the witch, but no one on the premises is to be shot."

Nash continued checking his weapon before reholstering it. He met Volkov's glare. "It's a tranq gun, dumbass."

Volkov opened his mouth to say something else, but Nash went out the back before he had a chance. Volkov swore. "If that asshole gets caught, I'm hanging him out to dry."

I didn't respond, watching Nash on the monitor. He sprinted for headquarters, avoiding the exterior camera like a pro, before disappearing around the side of the building.

Less than ten minutes later, he reappeared with an unconscious Gwen slung over his shoulders. I opened the back doors before he reached them. He didn't break stride, just ducked and leapt inside. He tapped the roof. "Move!"

Volkov clenched his jaw so hard my molars hurt watching him, but he threw the van in drive and took off as Nash lowered Gwen to the van floor. She was out cold, but he'd still zip tied her wrists and ankles and put a black hood over her head. I bit my lip as I studied her.

Nash noticed my guilt and softened his voice. "She'll be fine. These precautions ensure no one got hurt in the extraction. Scared people do unpredictable things."

I kept my eyes on the road and suffered through the tense silence during the drive.

Instead of going to a location Gwen could identify, Volkov parked behind Howl, one of his businesses. In addition to being the local alpha, he was also the CEO of Volkov Industries, Inc., which owned and operated a variety of businesses, including a five-story haunted house in the West Bottoms area of Kansas City. Along with several other haunted houses, Howl was a huge tourist draw during the Halloween season.

Staffed mostly by supernaturals, it was the one time of year when we didn't have to worry about hiding our natures. The tourists couldn't get enough of our incredible costumes and showmanship. *If they only knew.* I'd worked a season or two myself—although never at Howl. The last thing I'd wanted was to give an alpha any kind of authority over me, even if Howl's pay was the most generous of the houses.

Because the haunted houses wouldn't open for a couple weeks, the area was deserted. With its blacked-out windows and industrial feel, the old warehouse was the perfect location for an impromptu interrogation. Dez shifted in his seat when Volkov killed the engine. I wasn't the only one uncomfortable with how this could play out. No matter how much I tried to convince myself that this was a necessary evil, I couldn't get the image of Gwen's tattered stuffed bear out of my head.

"Careful," I said, as Nash picked up Gwen's prone body.

Other than a couple half-hearted whimpers and a finger twitch, Gwen hadn't stirred on the ride over. Nash nodded, cradling her against his chest rather than tossing her over a shoulder. I mouthed a thank you and opened the back doors for him.

Volkov directed us to a first-floor room that was already set up with a solitary metal table and a single bulb light. Once Howl opened for the season, this room would include an old-fashioned dentist chair and a tray of torture implements for the mad dentist exhibit, but for now, it served our purposes.

Dez and I watched from the door as Nash used his knife to cut through the zip tie on Gwen's wrists before securing her arms to the chair with new ones. Because Dez was far too kindhearted, both Nash and Volkov banned him from the room. Dez took one look at Gwen, paled, and said he'd wait in the van.

I moved to step inside the room, but Volkov blocked the opening. "Wait out there with Dez, Riley."

I braced my hands on my hips. "Absolutely not. Partners, remember?"

When he didn't budge, I put both palms against his chest and pushed—not that it did much good. It was like trying to move a boulder. "Move, Max."

"Trust me. You don't want to be in here." Volkov ran a hand across the back of his neck. "You're not going to like the version of me that will be in that room." He searched my face.

I knew all about hiding a version of yourself that you'd rather keep buried. I slid my palms up to the collar of his suit jacket and tugged him closer. This time, he didn't resist. "I don't scare easily."

Volkov stiffened. "You've never seen me like this."

I met his eyes. "I've lived with evil, and you're not it, regardless of the show you have to put on in there."

With a heavy sigh, Volkov stepped aside, allowing me to enter the room.

CHAPTER 18

For the next five minutes, Volkov and Nash bickered over who would do the questioning. Nash crossed his arms over his chest and leaned against the wall while Volkov paced the room waiting for Gwen to wake up. "Listen," Nash said, "you might be used to calling the shots in the boardroom, but you're out of your depth in here."

Volkov moved within striking distance of Nash and bared his teeth. "You have no idea what I've done."

Nash didn't flinch, even with an angry werewolf in his face. *Impressive.* I congratulated myself on the stellar recruiting choice while the two of them had their stare-off.

Nash continued to look at Volkov like he was something unsavory stuck to the bottom of his shoe. "I can tell you never served in the military, and while you dress like you belong in the FBI, I'd wager you've never worked there either. Conducting an interview and an interrogation are not remotely the same thing."

"Where I learned interrogation makes the FBI and the Army feel like story time." Volkov let his wolf peer through his eyes, the amber eerie in the barely lit room. "The only reason you're here is because I allow it. Don't push me."

I tried to diffuse the situation by pointing at Nash. "Tell you what. You play good cop." I tapped Volkov's shoulder. "And you can be bad cop."

Before either of them could snipe at the other again, Gwen began to stir. I reached for the black hood she still wore, but Volkov caught my hand. "Not yet."

Nash nodded his approval. At least the two agreed on something.

I positioned myself near the door, so I'd have a clear view of Gwen's face during questioning. I might not have the interrogation chops of either of the men in this room, but I was damn good at reading people. If Gwen lied, I was confident I'd pick up on it.

After several minutes of silence, Gwen's heart rate increased, and her breathing became labored. "Please," she croaked, shaking. "Let me go."

They let several more minutes tick by until it was all I could do to keep from interceding. At Volkov's nod, Nash stepped behind her and removed the hood. She must have been sleeping when he nabbed her because she wasn't wearing her glasses. I wondered how well she could see without them. Instead of moving back to the side, Nash remained where he was, his presence at her back a threat in itself.

Gwen blinked rapidly before her gaze locked on Volkov. I saw the second she realized who he was. "You." Apparently, her eyesight was good enough to recognize the threat in front of her.

Volkov smiled, but there was nothing friendly about it. "Me." He prowled closer, his eyes flashing amber again. "Did you really think that gaggle of witches would be enough to keep you safe from me?"

She swallowed audibly and struggled against her bonds. Nash dropped a heavy hand on her shoulder, and she froze. Gwen looked to me, her eyes pleading, but she was too afraid to speak. I tried my best to keep the sympathy off my face, but her desperation was choking the room. It was all I could do not to reassure her that everything would be fine.

Volkov tsked. "You're not going to make this more unpleasant than it needs to be, are you, Ms. Reynolds?"

Gwen rapidly shook her head. "No," she breathed. "I'll tell you whatever you want."

Volkov smiled. "I thought you might." He crouched down until they were at eye level. "Now tell me about the artifact."

"What artifact?" Gwen seemed genuinely confused.

"Don't play games," Volkov warned. "Where's the demon artifact?"

Gwen frowned. "I don't know anything about a demon artifact." She looked back to me. "You've got to believe me."

Volkov snapped his fingers in front of her face. "Eyes on me, Ms. Reynolds."

She obeyed immediately.

"Let's try this again." This time, he let the alpha command punctuate his words. "Tell me what you know about the demon artifact."

"I don't know anything. I swear." Her wide green eyes were bright with fear now.

Without realizing it, I took a step closer. Only the sharp shake of Nash's head stopped me.

Volkov moved so fast I didn't track him until his hand closed around Gwen's throat, the tips of his claws pressed hard enough against the tender skin of her neck to draw blood. I gasped, and Volkov stiffened, but he didn't let go.

It wasn't the threat to Gwen that shocked me. It was the partial shift. I'd been around a lot of shifters in my life, and I'd never known anyone capable of it. I didn't even know it was possible. The power and control needed to achieve and hold a partial shift was unheard of, relegated to campfire stories and tall tales. I gaped at Volkov.

This time, Nash moved to intercede, and I was the one warning him with a shake of my head. He scowled but halted, watching Volkov with wary eyes. I wondered if he'd been fooled by the expensive suit into believing Volkov was no more dangerous than the average man. If so, the wolf's claws extending from the crisp white sleeve of Volkov's dress shirt put that delusion to rest.

Gwen let out a strangled cry, her eyes bright with tears. "Please," she begged. "I would never go near demon magic. I can't tell you what I don't know."

Volkov's arm flexed, the tips of his claws digging in a little deeper. But Gwen didn't change her tune, even with terror coursing through her veins. Nash tensed and crowded closer to Gwen, prepared to pry Volkov's hands off if he took it too far.

But I knew Volkov. There were lines he wouldn't cross, and hurting a woman bound to a chair was one of them. A few seconds later, he proved me right, releasing his hold on Gwen's neck. She slumped in her chair and closed her eyes. Nash dropped his hands to his side and stepped back.

I believed Gwen. That kind of surprised reaction was hard to fake. But if she knew nothing about the artifact we were after, why did she go to Isaac for the kind of ritual ingredients used in coercion spells? I walked to Volkov's side, ignoring the annoyance radiating off him as I closed in.

"If you don't know anything about the artifact, why did you run when we mentioned Isaac?" I asked Gwen.

She fidgeted. Whatever the reason she went to see him, she wasn't keen on sharing.

"Well?" I prompted.

Gwen glanced at Volkov and slumped in her chair. "I bought illegal ingredients from him. I thought I was in trouble."

"What ingredients?" Volkov cut in.

Her cheeks flushed, and she mumbled her answer. I leaned closer and motioned for her to repeat it. She cleared her throat and listed her ingredients—none of which were in the photos of the ritual sites Volkov showed us. I frowned. "What kind of spell are those used for?"

She turned even redder. "A hex."

"A hex?" I repeated. "Who were you hexing?"

Gwen sat up straighter, pressing her lips into a thin line. "That's personal."

I laughed. "You're tied to a chair. Consider us on personal sharing territory if you want to get out of it."

She deflated. "Fine. My ex. He was a real jerk and emptied my bank account."

I raised an eyebrow.

"And he peed on my plants!" Outrage was stamped all over her pretty features. When Volkov gaped, she got defensive. "I caught it all on the nanny cam I hid next to the TV."

"The nanny cam?" Volkov asked.

"My plants kept dying. I never kill plants."

"Okay," I said, trying to get us back on productive ground. "And the shooter? Do you think that was the ex?"

Gwen rolled her eyes, losing some of her wariness now that both Volkov and Nash had backed off the intimidation tactics. "No. The only gun Tommy would pick up is in a video game. And even then, he's an awful shot."

"And you have no idea who would shoot at you?" Nash asked, joining the conversation.

"Me?" She practically squeaked as she tried to peer over her shoulder at Nash.

He stepped back, ensuring she didn't get a good look at him. *Smart man.*

"No one would shoot at me." Gwen swiveled back to Volkov. "I assumed they were you trying to kill you."

I bumped Volkov with my hip. "He gets that a lot."

When we were all satisfied that Gwen didn't know any more about the shooter or the artifact, Nash pulled up his balaclava to conceal his face and stepped out of the room. Volkov and I followed him out, assuring Gwen we'd cut her loose in a few minutes.

Volkov cleared his throat. "Are we good?" He held himself rigidly, as if sure that now that I'd seen him in that room, I wouldn't want to be near him.

I was a hugger, so I wrapped my arms around his waist and gave him a reassuring squeeze. "We're good."

Nash looked at us, shook his head, and headed for the door.

I turned in Volkov's arms, but he didn't release me. "Can you send Dez in?" I asked Nash before he could duck out. When his only answer was a grunt, I tried again. "We need Dez to compel Gwen to forget all about our little unauthorized chat," I said, keeping the growing irritation out of my tone.

Nash stalked out without a word. I guess I'd have to wait

to see if he did as I asked. I stared after Nash's retreating back. "I need Dez and Nash to work together."

Volkov pulled me closer and tugged my ponytail until my head tipped back. "Look. I get it. You want to be fair, for them to like you." He stared down at me. "You don't have to do any of this, you know. You don't have anything to prove." I tried to pull away, but he didn't let me retreat. When I remained stiff, he exhaled. "But if you are going to do this, then do it. You can't be fun Riley. You've got to lead. Stop asking them and start telling them what to do."

"That's not the only way to lead," I insisted. Not for me. I'd spent too many years under Carl's thumb to ever want to take his place.

"Maybe. But like it or not, that's how shit gets done." Volkov finally dropped his arms, and I stepped away.

I didn't argue because Volkov wasn't the one I needed to convince.

While we waited for Nash and Dez to come back, I mentally replayed the memory Isaac had shown me. Although Gwen had been vivid in the memory, I hadn't actually seen the blood-fire tourmaline crystal. I'd just assumed that she had been the one to buy it. Otherwise, why would Isaac show me Gwen in the first place? I frowned, trying to piece it together.

"I need to ask Gwen a question," I said.

Volkov followed me into the room.

"What was with the creepy mask you wore at Isaac's shop?" I asked her. In the memory Isaac showed me, it was definitely Gwen in that gilded mask.

Gwen startled. "The golden one?" She continued to stare at me in confusion as if trying to figure out how I could know that.

"When we went to him to trace some rare ingredients used

it in a ritual, Isaac showed me the memory of you wearing that mask. That's why we believed you were involved." Since Dez was going to wipe her memory, I saw no harm in sharing.

Gwen shook her head. "That doesn't make any sense. Why would he show you a memory of me wearing that mask? I only put in on because he asked me to."

"He played us. I knew that guy was squirrely." I caught Volkov's gaze. "He must have pulled up a random memory to throw us off."

Volkov clenched his fists. "This whole time. He's the witch we're after."

"Do you think he's our shooter?" I asked.

"I assumed the shooter had followed us," he said, "but if it was Isaac, it would explain how the shooter knew we were there."

"I can have Dez dig into his background. See if there's anything in there that would indicate he's a good enough shot to be our guy," I offered.

"Don't bother." Volkov's expression turned dangerous. "I'm going to pay him a visit myself. I'll find out."

"We," I corrected.

Volkov didn't respond.

"Partners, remember? If Isaac's our guy, he has the artifact I'm after or knows where it is." When he still didn't answer, I poked him in the chest. "I'm going."

CHAPTER 19

Only one of the three men who helped with the abduction stayed off my shit list. Nash ditched us the second he passed my message to Dez, claiming his part was done. *So much for teamwork.* Worse, Volkov slunk out while Dez and I escorted Gwen to the van, leaving us to transport her to coven headquarters where Dez replaced her memory of the evening's festivities with a rollicking memory of sneaking out for a night of too much beer and mechanical bull riding. The bull was my idea.

"Maybe he had pack business to take care of," Dez suggested, pulling the van out of the parking lot where we'd dropped Gwen.

I shot him an incredulous look. "Right. You and I both know he took the first opportunity to go after Isaac on his own. That man wouldn't know how to be a good partner if you gave him lessons." I shouldn't be surprised. Just because we had a few moments where we seemed to be connecting didn't change who he was. Max Volkov was an alpha, and well-intentioned or not, he steamrolled over his team the second it suited him.

I checked the time. It was shortly after midnight. "Screw this. We're going after Isaac ourselves." If Volkov wanted to go maverick on us, we'd do this job without him. He wasn't part of my team, anyway. I indicated the back of the van with my thumb. "We've got all the equipment we need to case the place. We'll find Isaac, figure out the best way to break into his shop, steal the artifact, and be done with this."

Dez held up his hand for a high five. I slapped his palm and then dug out my phone. When I dialed Nash's number, Dez's enthusiasm dimmed.

I held my hand over the phone. "Come on. We're a team, Dez. We all have a role here." I pointed in the direction of City Market. "Let's go see if Isaac is at his shop. There was a bed there, so I'm pretty sure he was sleeping on site."

He turned the van around. "Whatever you say."

I wasn't sure if that response was about the direction we were headed or the idea of us as a team. I let it go.

Nash finally picked up. "What?"

"Your phone manners are atrocious," I scolded.

"What do you want now?" Nash asked.

I told him what we learned about Isaac and about our plan to strike tonight if we got the opportunity. "Can you meet us there?"

Nash didn't answer right away. "What do you need me to do?"

I scowled down at my phone. "I don't know yet. Until we get eyes on the target, we can't formulate a plan."

"Well, call me when you have one, kid. My job is to bust heads or blow shit up." Nash hung up before I could object.

This is not how I imagined our first job going. I dropped my head to the dash with a thunk.

Dez nudged my shoulder. "Hey, we don't need Nash, either. We've got this."

I appreciated being able to count on him, so I didn't comment on the relief evident in Dez's voice that Nash wasn't coming. Eventually though, this team would have to gel if we were going to succeed. A two-man crew might get lucky a time or two, but in the larger scheme of things, it was a liability in this kind of work. I might be scrappy and Dez might be hitting the gym, but without more muscle than the two of us brought, it would only be a matter of time before we got caught. Or worse. We needed Nash's skill set, even if Dez would never admit it.

We spotted Volkov's car as soon as we turned onto the street in front of City Market. "That jerk," I grumbled.

Dez pulled in behind the overpriced Audi. "Want to let the air out of his tires?" he asked.

I grinned. This was why I loved Dez. "Yes. But we have more important things to do." I wouldn't stoop to petty pranks—no matter how tempting.

Dez shut off the van, unbuckled, and climbed in the back. He was already turning on equipment when I joined him. He scanned the building, focusing on the area where Isaac's shop was located. "There's one heat signature here." He pointed to a spot that was midway between where we were parked and Isaac's shop. "But if Volkov is in the building, it's probably him." He scanned the surrounding area. "The rest of the place is a ghost town."

At this time of night, it should be deserted. Either Isaac had an apartment somewhere else and the bed I saw was for napping, or our visit had spooked him, and he'd taken off already. "Can you hack into the security feed in the main aisle?" I hadn't seen a camera in the shop itself, but maybe we could see something useful.

Dez looked insulted. "Of course, I can." He turned his attention to the other monitor and a few minutes later cycled through the security feed. Nothing.

I threaded my hands behind my head and closed my eyes, thinking of the smart move. Without Isaac on site, it would be an ideal time to break into the shop and poke around. I doubted Isaac would be careless enough to leave a demon artifact unattended, but there might still be clues that could help us track it down.

If it were a normal business, I'd go in tonight without hesitation. But it wasn't a normal business. As a witch, Isaac would have set wards. If I tripped them, I'd lose the element of surprise. I could always enlist Janis's help to detect and dismantle them. She was an absolute whiz when it came to wards. She was also in her seventies and sound asleep at this time of night.

The sound of a fist on the side of the van made me jump. Volkov yanked the back doors open and scowled at Dez and I, like we were the ones who had ditched him. I glared back at him, wishing I would have let the air out of his tires when I had the chance.

Instead of joining us in the van, he stood with the doors open, letting in the cold September air. "Close the door," I snapped.

He continued to stand there with the doors open. "You might as well go home. There's no way into the shop tonight."

Even though I'd already decided I wasn't going to break in tonight, I resented him warning me off. "Not your business."

Volkov looked like he was going to argue but thought better of it. "The entrance is gone."

"What do you mean it's gone?" I asked.

"I assume he used some kind of cloaking spell, but since none of us are witches, we're not getting in there tonight."

I turned to Dez. "Oh, now there's a we. Isn't that convenient?"

Volkov tapped on the door. "Go home, Riley."

"Piss off, Max."

His phone rang, cutting off whatever retort was on the tip of his tongue. "Slow down, Ward."

I didn't have Dez's vampire hearing, so I couldn't quite make out the other end of the conversation. Whatever was going on, it must be bad. Craig Ward wasn't a man prone to rushing anything. The Kansas City enforcer was the poster boy for stone cold efficiency.

"We're on our way." Volkov hung up.

"What is it?" I asked.

"She's okay, but Kali was attacked tonight."

Dez tossed me my jacket. "Go."

I beat Volkov to his car and waited for him to unlock my door. "Who attacked her?"

"That's what we're going to find out." His foot was heavy on the gas as we raced toward West Bottoms.

For once, I was grateful that Volkov thought speed limits didn't apply to him.

CHAPTER 20

Kali sat on her couch, while a furious gargoyle pressed a bag of frozen blueberries to her head. She swatted Craig's hand away. "My head is fine." Reluctantly, he tossed the blueberries to the coffee table, but he didn't take his eyes off her. Kali was wearing champagne colored silk pajamas that belted at the waist, her dark hair curling around her shoulders. Even after taking a blow to the head, she managed to look glamorous.

I shuffled past Craig and sat beside her, pulling her in for a hug. Craig let me pass but crossed his big arms over his chest and stood sentinel. "What happened?" I asked her.

Kali shrugged. "I don't know. I was here alone. One minute I was in the kitchen setting up the coffee maker for morning and the next thing I knew, I woke up with a bump." She pointed to a spot on the crown of her head.

"I found her on the floor unconscious." Craig's voice was rough, a muscle working in his jaw.

"Someone hit you from behind, then?" Volkov clarified.

Kali frowned. "Maybe. I don't know."

I squeezed her hand. "What is the last thing you remember?"

She rubbed her temples. "There was a cloying sweet smell, almost floral." Kali touched her lips. "And I had this sudden bitter taste on my tongue. That's the last thing I remember before waking up on the kitchen floor with Craig crouched down beside me."

"Was anything taken?" Volkov asked.

She shook her head. "No. Nothing. It doesn't make any sense. Why would someone break in, knock me out, and then just leave?"

Craig's whole body tensed, like he was ready to go to battle. His frustration at feeling powerless wasn't hard to read. Volkov clapped a hand onto his shoulder. "We'll find whoever did this."

"Is there anything else?" I asked. "Anything you saw or heard that could give us a clue?"

While there were plenty of people gunning for me, I couldn't think of anyone with a grudge against Kali—at least no one still alive. Although Kali looked like a pinup girl, she'd been training hardcore for a year and could handle herself. Between her new fighting skills and her overprotective gargoyle boyfriend, most people would leave her alone. Whoever this was either was familiar enough with her skill set to recognize the need to knock her out from behind or they got lucky. But why go to all that trouble, and then take nothing? The attacker had to be after something.

Kali closed her eyes as if replaying the moments leading up to the attack. She tilted her head. "Right before I passed out, there was this brief flash of gold. That's the last thing I recall before waking up."

Something heavy settled in my stomach. "Something

gold?" I had assumed whatever happened here was unrelated to the trouble we were stirring up, but now I wasn't so sure. "Like a watch?"

"Could be. It was just a flash." Kali sagged against the couch cushions. "I'm sorry. That's not very helpful."

Craig sat on the other side of her and tucked her under his arm. I stood and crossed the room to Volkov.

He picked up on my unease. "What is it?"

"When Helen and I went to see Isaac, he was wearing some kind of watch or bracelet. I didn't get a close look, but I did notice the flash of gold at his wrist when he moved."

"It might not be related. Isaac would have no reason to come after Kali. But," he reassured me, "we'll check into it."

Something told me that we didn't include me, but I wouldn't be dismissed that easily. "My gut says it's related."

Kali pulled away from Craig. "Then we follow your gut. Now, who's Isaac?"

While Volkov got them up to speed, I called Helen. Her voice was sleepy, reminding me that it was nearing dawn. It had been one hell of a long night.

"What's wrong?" Helen asked.

"I'm fine," I said, knowing she'd assume the worst. "You remember those spell ingredients that we were looking into for Volkov?"

"Yes. Why?" she asked.

"You said Devil's Snare was a hallucinogen, right? That it could be used for coercion and memory alteration?"

"That's right."

"Could it be used to knock someone out? Make them forget what happened?" I asked.

"Sure," she agreed. "What's going on, hon?"

I explained the attack on Kali as well as my suspicions. It

was possible that something spooked whoever knocked Kali out, and the perp ran. But if my hunch was right, and it was Isaac, then he was after something. There was a chance Kali saw more than she realized. If we could access her subconscious memory of the event, maybe we'd get some answers.

"Do you remember enough of that memory retrieval spell to repeat it?" I asked Helen.

"Yeah. I think so."

I turned to Kali and explained how the spell worked. "Are you willing to try the memory retrieval spell?"

She didn't hesitate. "Let's do it."

Something rustled in the background, like Helen was getting dressed. "Do you want to come now?"

I glanced at everyone's tired expressions. Kali looked about ready to drop. Even if we got answers now, we were all too exhausted to go after Isaac. Without sleep, we'd make mistakes we couldn't afford. "No. It can wait for a few hours while we all get some sleep."

We agreed to meet in the afternoon to try the spell. Because Volkov's place was a thirty-minute drive, and the man was dead on his feet, I convinced him to crash at my place.

I tried not to feel self-conscious about the sad state of my apartment. Colorful throw pillows could only do so much to make a place like this look homey. Between the peeling lead paint and the chipped kitchen cabinets, my apartment was falling apart. It would probably be the shittiest place he'd ever slept. Not that he let on.

Volkov kept his gaze on me as I pulled a spare set of sheets from the tiny hall closet and grabbed the extra pillow off my bed for the futon. "Let me help with that," he offered, taking the pile from my hands.

Everything in this apartment, I'd found, fixed, or bargained for. And with its duct tape patch and faded fabric, the futon looked every bit the salvaged piece of furniture it was. I'd snagged it from behind the dumpster when my downstairs neighbor moved and left it behind. Prior to that, I had plastic lawn chairs in my living room and an inflatable couch that popped as soon as I sat on it. Worst twenty bucks I ever spent, and that was saying something. At the time, the futon had been a definite upgrade.

I stared at Volkov as he unfolded the futon into a bed. There was nothing level about that mattress. He'd probably roll off in the middle of the night. "You know what," I said. "On second thought, you should sleep on the bed."

"This is great," he insisted. He finished wrangling the fitted sheet on it and sat gingerly on the edge. His eyes widened when the janky leg gave out and one side sagged several more inches.

"I'm going to buy a new couch," I blurted out. "When I get paid for this job, I'm going to that big warehouse furniture store over by Legends that sells everything, and I'm buying the fluffiest, most level sectional they have. This one is just temporary." I knew I was babbling, but the longer I looked at him sitting on my crappy couch in a suit that cost more than my rent, the more I babbled.

"Good," he said, his pale blue eyes earnest. "You deserve nice things, Riley."

Maybe it was the adrenaline crash or just my exhaustion, but his words tipped me over the edge. I'd never been a pretty crier, and from Volkov's horrified expression, I was guessing tonight was not the exception. The thought made me cry harder.

Volkov stood up, despite having to fight the wobbly futon

to get to his feet, and pulled me against his chest. He rubbed a hand up and down my back and murmured comforting words against my hair. By the time I was cried out, the entire front of his dress shirt was wet, and I had to run to the bathroom for a tissue before I snotted all over his chest. I splashed water on my blotchy face before forcing myself to go back out there and face him.

"I don't know what that was," I said with a sniffle.

He'd taken off his jacket and shoes while I'd been hiding out in the bathroom, and he looked like some kind of billionaire playboy. I must have looked like I was on the verge of another bout of tears because Volkov wrapped an arm around my shoulders and steered me toward my bedroom. "Come on. You need sleep."

When he turned to go back to the futon, I grabbed his arm and tugged him toward the bed. I kicked off my shoes, peeled off my jeans, and crawled under the comforter. He only paused a second before climbing into the bed beside me fully dressed. Within minutes, I was asleep.

When I woke hours later, my legs were tangled in the sheet and a warm arm was banded around my waist, Volkov's steady breathing in my ear. I closed my eyes again, letting the sound lull me, and for a few precious minutes before I fell back to sleep, I pretended things could be different between us.

CHAPTER 21

The next day, my hunch proved right. Seconds after Helen performed the blood magic spell in Kali's living room, I watched the memory of Isaac bending over Kali, the blood-fire tourmaline crystal clutched in his hand. His lips moved, and although I couldn't make out the full incantation, I caught enough to know what he was after. I watched Isaac pull the memory from Kali's head, saw it coalesce like smoke and wrap around the crystal before it absorbed the memory, glowing hellfire red under the fluorescent kitchen lights.

Isaac tucked the crystal into his pocket and stood. I caught that familiar flash of gold again. This time, his sleeve pulled up enough to expose the object. That wasn't a watch he wore on his wrist. It was a gold cuff shaped like a striking serpent, the snake's eyes made of a glowing yellow stone that looked a lot like sulfur.

I didn't need an illustration to know what I was looking at. Valac's artifact had been right under my nose the whole time I sat across from Isaac. By the time Kali's memory faded, my heart was racing with the implications.

I recounted Kali's memory in detail.

"You said Isaac stole a memory from Kali," Volkov said. "Did he say what the memory was?"

"No." I went over everything again, concentrating to pick up anything I missed. I leaned forward. "Wait. He said something about a tracing spell." I'd glossed right over that, thinking he meant a memory tracing spell. But what if that wasn't what he'd meant?

From Volkov's swearing, I guessed I was right. "Does that mean something?"

Kali, Craig, and Volkov all exchanged worried looks. Craig was the one to lay it out for me. "Kali and I found a blood-tracing spell several months ago. It disappeared along with the demon who used it." When Kali paled, he pulled her closer to reassure her. "It was an exceedingly dangerous spell because it allowed whoever used it to trace any bloodline. There are a lot of people who would kill to get their hands on something like that. And none of them are the good guys."

I let that sink in. "And that spell would be stored in both of your memories?" I guessed.

"It would," Craig admitted.

"Let me get this straight," I said, dread pooling in my stomach. "Isaac now has a demon artifact capable of controlling someone and a spell that would allow him to hunt down anyone he wants?"

"He'd need a blood sample from a descendent, but yes," Craig said.

Volkov launched into action, grabbing his keys from where he'd tossed them and heading for the door. "We need to find Isaac." He paused next to Helen. "Get your witches down to City Market now. I want that cloaking spell disarmed as soon as possible." He left without waiting for input or acknowledgement.

He was right that we didn't have time to waste, but we'd only get one shot at this. If he flushed Isaac out of his hiding spot, we risked losing him—and the artifact he wore—for good. Going in hot might be Volkov's style, but it wasn't going to work in this instance. Not with Valac's mind-control trinket on Isaac's wrist. The last thing we needed was for Isaac to gain control of a powerful witch like Helen, or worse, an alpha werewolf capable of shifting to claw or fang on command. I shuddered imagining the devastation Isaac could cause with either of them under his control.

That cloaking spell would come down alright, but first, we needed a viable plan for retrieving the artifact. Volkov might not like it, but it was the right play. While Kali and Craig went into damage control mode, I pulled Helen aside to get her promise that no one would bring down that spell until I was ready.

Because I didn't have time to waste on multiple phone calls, the situation called for extreme measures.

I set up a group text for my team.

After a moment's hesitation, I added Volkov to the group. He might be high-handed, but that didn't mean I had to be. We needed everyone cooperating to pull this off. I typed out a quick text briefing the team on the situation and the risks. Because there was a quilt blocking class today at the Stitch Witch, we couldn't meet there. Although it was far from ideal, I asked everyone to meet me at my apartment in two hours to plan the heist. Then I crossed my fingers and hoped they'd all show up.

My apartment was better suited to peddling illegal substances than hosting a planning session, but sometimes, you had to work with what you had. Dez and I were camped out on my lopsided futon, while Helen claimed the lone armchair. Between the bump to the head and the after-effects of the memory retrieval spell, Kali was at her place trying to sleep off the world's worst headache. Volkov and Craig stood with their backs to the wall, and Nash was yet to show.

Dez bent close to me. "He's not coming."

"Try not to sound so happy about it," I grumbled.

"Sorry." He passed me the bag of corn nuts he'd brought as a peace offering.

My nerves were too strained to enjoy snack food. Volkov glanced at his watch—again—before sending me a pointed look.

"Fine," I muttered. "We'll start without him."

We went over what we knew. Before coming over, Helen had checked out the cloaking spell on Isaac's shop and was confident she could break it. She cautioned us not to assume that Isaac wasn't holed up inside. According to Helen, that spell was powerful enough to shield him from showing up on infrared imaging.

Although we couldn't assume Creed was involved in this, we couldn't rule it out either. Both the blood-tracing spell and the cuff of Valac would fetch unbelievable amounts of money at auction. If Isaac had Creed's backing, it would make him even more volatile. With those kinds of connections, Creed could send in mercenaries to ensure Isaac made it out of Kansas City with the artifact. If that were the case, the sooner we moved to secure Isaac, the better.

Dez had just finished going over the building layout and schematics for Isaac's shop when Nash showed up, letting himself in without knocking. I hadn't bothered to lock my door or reactivate the alarm after Dez arrived since it seemed pointless. Volkov shot me a disappointed look, which I ignored.

"Nice place." Nash picked up the lava lamp he'd tampered with when he broke into my apartment last month, then eyed the state-of-the-art security system Volkov had installed with a shake of his head. "You know that fancy alarm is useless against anyone who wants in here bad enough, right?"

Of course, I did, but since it made Volkov feel better, I kept it.

Nash walked the room as if inspecting it and finding it lacking. *That makes two of us, buddy.* "At least you'll be able to afford a decent place once we get paid for that artifact."

Volkov gave Nash a dirty look. "Watch yourself."

I headed off the trouble. "Dez? Can you go over everything for Nash?"

After a heavy sigh, Dez ran us through the market's physical security features and access points again. When he finished, he turned it over to Helen, who outlined the magical security features she'd noted when we visited Isaac. The wards themselves were rudimentary, so once the cloaking spell was down, disabling them shouldn't pose much of a challenge.

"Okay," I said. "We'll go in at night when we have the best chance of catching Isaac unaware."

"I say we go now," Volkov countered.

Craig frowned, no doubt imagining the goose egg Isaac had given Kali as a parting gift, and nodded. "Max and I will go in first and secure the witch. Then Riley can get her artifact."

I huffed in annoyance. "That's not going to work. We can't risk Isaac using the cuff to control either of you."

"It'll be hard to use it when he's unconscious," Craig promised.

"And if he uses it before you get to him? Then what?" I asked. "How many of us are you willing to risk? Can you live with yourself if he uses you to kill us?"

"The kid's right," Nash said. "Going in at night is the smart move." He tipped his hat to Helen. "Ma'am. How long will it take you to disable the spell?"

Helen beamed at his show of deference. "Ten minutes, give or take," she said.

"There are no cameras aimed at the entrance," Dez said. "And I can bypass any of the others in case he's tapped in."

"Will he know when the cloaking spell drops?" I asked Helen.

Helen nodded. "Yeah. If he set it himself, he'll feel it as soon as it drops."

Nash walked over to the printouts strewn across my coffee table and picked up the one with the building access points labeled. He tapped on the sky light.

I smiled. "Exactly what I was thinking."

Nash studied the drawings. "Two people could rappel in from here in a matter of seconds once that cloaking spell drops."

"That's what I would do." Helen stretched her legs. "If these old knees were younger, I'd join you myself."

"I'm sure you would," Nash said. He looked at Dez. "Can you pinpoint his location with that fancy equipment of yours once there's no magical interference?"

Dez gave him the stink eye. "Of course."

"Good. I'm assuming you have comms?"

"We do," I answered before Dez lost his temper. "But I don't think we should wait around for confirmation of his location. Every second counts. Hopefully, he'll be sound asleep here." I pointed to a spot on the drawing where the bed was located.

"And if he's not?" Volkov demanded.

"If he's not, we'll have eyes on him through the skylight." Neither Volkov nor Craig were fans of this plan, so I threw them a bone. "Give us a sixty-second head start, then the two of you can bust through the front door and cause a commotion."

Volkov snatched the drawing from my hand and glared down at it. "A lot can happen in sixty seconds."

I cracked my knuckles. "That's the point."

"Fine," Volkov bit out. "But I'll be the one going in with you."

"Like hell you will," Nash objected. "Last I checked, she hired me for the job."

"He's right. Nash has plenty of rappelling experience." I hoped that was true. "This is exactly the kind of thing he trained for." Nash snorted but didn't correct me.

I pointed to the front entrance on the drawing. "You'll be right there. That's going to have to be good enough."

Nash didn't stick around for consensus. I jumped to my feet before he could escape. "Wait! I have something for you." I grabbed the bags I'd stashed in the kitchen and thrust them into his hands.

As soon as he realized I'd handed him chicken feed and premium black soldier fly larvae treats, he tried to give the bags back. "I'm not keeping the rooster."

I opened the door and shoved him out, bags in hand. I'd never met anyone who needed a pet as much as that man did.

CHAPTER 22

The last time I rappelled through a skylight, I'd been fifteen years old and on a job for Carl. He'd sent me after an amulet that was allegedly spelled for good fortune. Naturally, I'd had nothing but crap luck from the time Carl dropped me at the site. My line was cut, leaving me stranded inside with a pair of angry vampires who thought I'd make a tasty midnight snack. After I made it out alive, I found out it had all been one of Carl's little tests. He wanted to see how well I could think on my feet. Rather than retrieving a rare artifact, he'd actually sent me in after a cheap piece of costume jewelry. One of the vampires owed Carl money, so he'd staged the whole thing as a favor. That hadn't stopped him from sinking his fangs into my leg while I was scrambling out his second-story window.

Tonight, I was surrounded by a team I'd hand-picked. That didn't mean trust came easily. When Nash tied us both off, I had to resist the urge to double and triple check his efforts.

Nash and I had been sprawled out on our bellies on this roof for the last hour, watching Isaac sleep. He slept like the

139

dead, with his arms crossed over his chest like he was tucked into a sarcophagus. *What a creep.*

I checked my watch. Three minutes until go time. We'd all synchronized our watches prior to assuming our positions. We also wore comms that would allow Helen to tell us the exact second the cloaking spell was down.

Nash turned his head toward me. "You ready?"

I nodded, trying not to fidget. The wait was always the worst, when every nerve ending was on high alert and the adrenaline was lighting me up.

Nash went over the hand signals again. He'd insisted on them—one for abort, another for hit the deck, and a third for trouble. The second we were on the roof, Nash's whole demeanor changed, and I got a glimpse of what he must have been like before the Army cut him loose.

I tapped my watch. "Two minutes."

That was Nash's cue to pull the pane he'd prepped for removal earlier. Thanks to the bank of single pane windows that made up Isaac's skylight, access was as easy as cutting through the seal and popping the lowest pane out. Nash set the glass aside, and we waited for Helen's all clear.

As planned, I went through first, dropping silently to the floor. I didn't turn to make sure Nash made it inside, rushing to the side of Isaac's bed and zeroing in on my prize. Although I'd assumed Isaac would take the demon relic off to sleep, he slept in the thing, which made the next step trickier.

I edged closer to the bed to study the artifact, searching for a clasp. I couldn't see one, which meant it must slide off like a bangle. That definitely complicated things. Valac's cuff was a golden serpent that coiled around Isaac's arm. The eyes glowed yellow even in the moonlit room, making the piece seem sentient. And that wasn't even the worst of it. Now that

I was close enough to inspect it, I could see where the serpent's fangs sank into the top of his wrist.

I caught Nash's eye and signaled for trouble before pointing to the cuff. He nodded and moved closer. Although we'd discussed using a magical knock-out potion, in the end, we hadn't wanted to wait the day it would cost us to brew it. Nash was more than happy to go old school. Within seconds, he had duct-taped Isaac's mouth to prevent him from issuing any commands and zip tied his ankles and wrists. Isaac's eyes flew open, his body straining against the palm Nash pinned against his chest.

I got to work. I didn't want to shred Isaac's arm, so I needed to pry the fangs out of his skin. As soon as I touched the artifact, the eyes glowed brighter. I forced myself not to yank my hand back, but I couldn't help the shudder as I tried to work it loose. Unfortunately, the fangs stayed embedded in his arm.

"Pull it off," Nash insisted.

I understood his urgency. The longer it took to get it off Isaac, the more we risked him gaining control of one of us. But the bracelet was fitted to Isaac's wrist tightly enough that I couldn't pull it free. I ran my hands along the body of the serpent, feeling for a hidden release. When I found none, I racked my brain for another option. Short of cutting off his hand, I wasn't sure how to get the damn thing off.

I wasn't about to saw through bone, but the thought did give me an idea. I pulled the dagger sheathed under my jacket. It was a wicked blade forged in hellfire. Literally. The demon artifact was one of two weapons capable of killing demons, and the Enclave had grudgingly allowed me to keep it when I took this job.

Since the blade was capable of taking out a demon, I hoped

that it could be used to cut through a golden cuff. Before I could try, Nash's hand shot out, capturing my wrist. "He'll bleed out."

"I'm not hacking off his hand." I wedged the tip of the blade under the head of the snake, hoping it would be enough to break the bite. Not only did the fangs release, the serpent uncoiled from his wrist the second the blade touched it, and it slithered across the back of my hand. I reacted on instinct, tossing it across the room and scrambling on top of the nearest chair.

"Really?" Nash shook his head in disgust and pointed to the artifact that had now reformed into the cuff.

"It moved," I said defensively. I climbed off the chair with as much dignity as I could muster and wrapped the cuff in my jacket. I tied the sleeves—just in case it decided to slither to life again.

Volkov must have lost patience because I heard a loud boom right before he and Craig thundered up the stairs. He'd given us considerably more than our negotiated sixty seconds though. Despite a few hiccups and a jump scare, this job went better than I'd expected. *Easiest hundred grand I'd ever make.* I offered Nash a fist bump, but he stared at my hand until I dropped it.

When I turned back to Isaac, he mumbled against the tape. Nash looked to me, and I shrugged. Might as well hear what he had to say now that there was no chance he could control us. Nash ripped the tape from his mouth as Volkov and Craig came up the stairs.

When Isaac spotted Volkov, he stopped struggling against his bonds. "Thank the goddess you're here." He pointed at Nash and me. "These two attacked me."

I snort-laughed. "Nice try."

Isaac sat up, scooting to the edge of his bed before rising on unsteady feet. "Who are you people?" he demanded, gazing around the room as if it were unfamiliar to him. "And where am I?"

Either Isaac was a world-class actor, or there was more to this demon relic than the information we'd been given. Even with three scary-ass men and Helen interrogating him, his story never wavered. According to Isaac, the last thing he remembered was going to meet a potential buyer who had inquired about the 1967 Chevrolet Impala he'd lovingly restored and listed for sale on Autotrader. The specificity of his lie gave me more pause than his insistence he'd never seen Valac's cuff before I showed it to him.

Fortunately, he'd already given us the means to see for ourselves. For the third time in a week, we'd use the blood magic spell to retrieve his memory. After getting burned with the memory of Gwen he'd shown me, we'd make sure to demand a full day's worth of memories though. The spell would take more blood to power because of the time span, but I wasn't willing to fall for Isaac's bait and switch twice.

CHAPTER 23

"Show me the day you received the serpent cuff," I said.

Whether Isaac was fighting the demand, or it truly was buried in his subconscious, it took a while for the memory to surface. By the time he showed me anything useful, my palm stung, and my blood colored the water red. At least Isaac didn't root around in my head like he had the first time we'd done this spell.

In Isaac's memory, I sat in a retro-styled diner across from a man I'd only seen in a photograph. Luca Cardelli had the same baby face, but he carried himself with the confidence of a man good at his job. He reached into his jacket pocket and pulled out a black velvet drawstring bag and sat it on the table between them.

Isaac stared at it. "Is that a down payment? I'm sorry, but I can't hold the car. Work has been slow, and I need the money, or I wouldn't be selling it."

It seemed like Isaac was telling the truth about thinking he had been meeting a buyer. Isaac seemed to genuinely want to sell his car.

Cardelli tilted his head, studying Isaac. "My client is in need of someone with your particular skill set."

"I don't really do restorations for other people. I'm just a hobbyist," Isaac protested.

"She's not interested in restoring a car," Cardelli assured him. "You have a reputation for being exceptionally skilled with memory manipulation spells."

Isaac shook his head. "I put all that behind me years ago. I don't do that anymore."

Cardelli continued as if Isaac hadn't just turned him down. "She's instructed me to give you a gift. Consider it a show of good faith," he said smoothly as he pushed the black velvet drawstring bag across the table toward Isaac.

"I can't help you," Isaac insisted. Since I was watching the scene through Isaac's eyes, I couldn't gauge his expression, but he sounded panicked. He didn't reach for the bag.

"Please," Cardelli said, indicating the bag. "It's quite valuable. A rare magical artifact. Take a closer look."

Isaac stood abruptly. "Who are you?"

"Just the messenger," Cardelli said, nodding at someone standing behind Isaac. "Let me introduce you to someone in need of your services."

When Isaac turned, a beautiful middle-aged woman with intense dark eyes and wild blonde hair stood in his path. She held her right hand out for the bag. A tattoo of a thorny vine twisted around her arm with a single blood-red rose blooming against the blue vein on her exposed wrist. As soon as Cardelli handed the bag to her, she dismissed him with a flick of her hand. "You may go." She kept her gaze on Isaac as Luca Cardelli walked away.

"Now then. Let's not make this unpleasant." She smiled, and the effect was chilling. I knew on an instinctual level that I was in the presence of a dangerous creature.

"I won't tell anyone," Isaac promised, sliding out of the booth.

"No. You won't." The woman dipped her hand into the velvet bag and pulled out a writhing golden snake by the neck.

Isaac scrambled back, but he wasn't fast enough. The viper struck, its fangs sinking into his wrist and its body coiling around Isaac's arm until it fused into the golden cuff.

The woman pushed back the loose sleeve of her shirt, exposing the matching cuff on her left arm. The serpent's eyes brightened against her pale skin, the eyes of Isaac's cuff glowing in response. She stroked the snake's head like it was a living thing, and Isaac's eyes went milky white before they returned to normal. He stilled and waited for the woman to speak.

"Now then," she said. "There's a blood-tracing spell I seek."

A wall of black slammed over my vision, snapping me out of the memory and back to the present. When I blinked away the darkness, Volkov's face was in front of mine, his hands gripping my shoulders as he shook me. It took several seconds for me to get my bearings again, the sound in the room coming back with a whoosh.

"Riley!" Volkov's voice was too loud, and I flinched. He let out a harsh breath and yanked me against the solid heat of his chest, wrapping his arms around me. I counted his heartbeats until my legs felt steady again and my head clear.

I stepped back, still trying to make sense of what I'd seen. "You shouldn't have pulled me out," I whispered.

Volkov frowned. "We didn't pull you out. You started to shake, and your eyes rolled back. I caught you before you hit the floor." He ran a hand through his hair and glared at Isaac, like his memory had harmed me on purpose.

Maybe it had. But there was more I needed to see. "I need to try again."

Volkov tensed, and his eyes shifted to his wolf. "No."

I turned to Helen, desperate to go back in. "I need to see the rest of that memory," I insisted.

She squared her thin shoulders and lifted her chin. "It's too dangerous."

Gritting my teeth, I mentally counted to calm myself. I didn't make it to six. "It's my choice." I scanned their faces, searching for an ally and finding nothing but worry and resolve. It was a rare moment of consensus, with even Nash on their side. Too bad it was at the expense of information we needed.

It took twenty minutes of arguing and threatening to go to another witch before Helen relented to try again. No amount of bargaining convinced them to let me be the one to go back into the memory though. Craig volunteered. Because getting the full memory was more important than winning the argument, I agreed.

Unfortunately, the memory fractured again, kicking Craig out the same as it had me. This time, it took both Nash and Volkov to catch him before he hit the floor. When he regained his equilibrium, we recounted identical memories.

I paced the room. "It's so little to go on." I rounded on Isaac who perched on the edge of one of the couches, looking shell-shocked. "Did you recognize the woman in the memory?"

His denial was instantaneous and convincing.

Craig interrupted before I could question him further. "I did." His grim expression said it wasn't good news.

"Who's behind this?" Volkov demanded.

We all collectively held our breath for Craig's answer.

He didn't keep us waiting. "Zara Bellarose."

Of all the names I'd been prepared for, hers hadn't been among them. But maybe it should have been. As one of three power brokers who ran the North American underground markets, she dealt in rare, forbidden magic as often as Damien Creed did. I'd been so fixated on the connection between Cardelli and Gwen and the possibility of Creed's involvement, I'd overlooked the other power players. I should have known better.

Bellarose was as powerful as Creed and rumored to be even more deadly. If you had the cash, Bellarose could hook you up with all manner of dangerous magical artifacts, but stepping into her orbit was like playing Russian roulette.

Of course, she'd want to get her hands on a blood-tracing spell. And with the whole of the Witches' Council aware of the spell's existence, it wasn't surprising that Bellarose could find and exploit a leak to get that information. Before rising to power as a forbidden magic broker, Bellarose had been an up-and-coming witch with more ambition than conscience. It had gotten her booted off the powerful Witches' Council. When she'd resurfaced a decade later, she'd amassed control of the underground market stretching from Canada down to the Midwest and across the East Coast.

This was the woman who'd paid Carl to steal the Alatyr stone, a magical artifact rumored to grant near immortality, from Damien Creed a decade ago. And now she'd acquired a demon artifact capable of controlling another person and a blood-tracing spell that would allow her to track down any supernatural she wanted as long as she had blood from a descendent. I had no idea what her end goal was, but it couldn't be good.

"This is really bad," I said in the understatement of the year, before telling everyone about the Carl connection.

No one acquired that much power without getting a lot of blood on their hands. And we were about to go after her. Maybe this wasn't shaping up to be such easy money, after all.

CHAPTER 24

Whenever I imagined running my own heists, I pictured a ragtag group of clever misfits bonding over holographic images and refreshments. There would be plush seating, ample donuts, and a cutthroat game of ping-pong to break up our planning sessions. I'd be living the dream.

Instead, I was squatting inside a porta-potty the day after we'd broken into Isaac's place because a water main break rendered the Stitch Witch bathroom unusable. Since my landlady threatened to call the cops the last time we congregated in my apartment, we'd been forced to find an alternative location to meet. Dez refused to invite Nash into his apartment, like some kind of reverse vampire paranoia. Nash's place was too far away. Although Volkov offered his library, I didn't want to muddy the waters. He might be on the group chat, but he wasn't a long-term member of the team. The Stitch Witch won by default, despite its non-functioning bathroom.

After an hour of strategizing, aka bickering, I was happy

for the reprieve, even if my hideout did smell rank enough to make my eyes water.

"Are you still in there?" Dez asked through the plastic wall. He knew I was. There was no hiding from a vampire.

I took a deep breath, immediately regretting it. "Coming." I poked my head out to find Dez waiting for me. "Is everyone still alive?"

"For now," he said. "But Helen threatened to crack some skulls if we didn't stop arguing."

I grinned. "Did it work?"

Dez scratched his cheek. "Surprisingly well. But it won't last."

No. It wouldn't. "I guess we better take advantage of the momentary truce then."

When we rejoined the others, Helen's body blocking the door was the only thing that prevented Nash from bolting. "Where are you going?" I asked.

"This is a waste of time. Call me when you've got something."

I planted a palm on his chest and pushed him toward a nearby stool. "Nash, we need everyone for this."

I held my breath until he sat down. It was a small win, but I had to keep the team from fracturing. He promptly leaned against the wall and pulled his baseball cap low over his eyes like he was about to take a nap. *Small win,* I reminded myself.

"Okay. What do we know?" I asked the room at large.

Volkov spoke first, rattling off general information about Bellarose's operation including the dates of upcoming auctions that Craig had dug up. While we were here strategizing, Craig and Kali were manning her new booth at the Kansas City Renaissance Festival. Although she'd offered to cancel, I convinced her to go. She'd been over-the-moon excited about the prospect of selling her gorgeous costumes at the festival since she scored the booth. I was happy to pull her in whenever we needed disguises, but I didn't want her putting her life on hold every time I had a job.

"According to Craig's intel, the auction coming up next month is most likely where she'd put the spell up for bid," Volkov said.

"If she's even planning to sell it," I countered. I wasn't convinced she didn't have bigger plans than a big payday.

Volkov tipped his chin in acknowledgement. "Either way, we've got the crystal."

After questioning Isaac, Craig took him to a safe house where Bellarose couldn't get to him—one with good locks and around-the-clock shifters on babysitting duty to prevent Isaac from running. The rest of us had canvassed Isaac's shop until we located the crystal. Thankfully, he hadn't had time to hand it over to Bellarose yet.

I reached for the blood-fire tourmaline that sat like a centerpiece in the middle of the worktable. "I say we hand over the crystal."

For the first time that morning, the room quieted. Only Helen nodded enthusiastically. She knew me well enough to know where I was headed with this. "That's a great idea," she said.

Everyone looked at us like we were nuts.

"Can you find another one of these?" I asked Helen.

"Yeah. But it's gonna cost a fortune," she warned.

"How much?" I asked. "I've got the fifty grand Sato deposited in my bank account."

"I'll cover it," Volkov said. When I started to object, he cut me off. "Save your money for that couch."

I swallowed past the sudden lump in my throat and

nodded. "Thank you." I sat the crystal back on the table, and then laid out the plan. "We'll get Isaac to transfer a mundane memory into the new crystal. Bellarose will have no way of knowing it's the wrong memory until it's too late. And while Isaac is handing over the crystal, I'll be swiping the cuff right off her arm."

"You think she'll come to him?" Volkov asked.

"She did before, so I think there's a good chance," I reasoned.

I looked at Dez. "Can you compel Isaac to hand it over without tipping Bellarose off?"

Rather than answering right away, he considered it. "I think so."

Nash snorted, and I kicked his chair.

"I'm confident you can do it, Dez," I assured him.

"How are you planning to get that cuff off her wrist without her noticing?" Nash jumped into the conversation, proving he was paying attention despite the heavy-lidded eyes.

Helen snatched Nash's baseball cap from his head and slapped him in the chest with it. "She's a damn fine pick-pocket. That's how." Helen said it with the pride most people reserved for their kids' trophies and advanced degrees.

When Nash recovered from his shock, he turned to me. "You do recall that Isaac's cuff didn't just slide off, right?"

I pulled out my dagger. "It did as soon as I touched it with this. All I need to do is brush up against the cuff and catch the snake when it slithers off her arm." I repressed the shudder at the thought. There were a lot of fears I'd overcome for a hundred grand. In this line of work, touching a golden snake would likely be the first of many.

Dez had already hacked into Isaac's burner phone and

found a message from Bellarose. Now that we had a plan, he sent a reply to arrange the drop. Within an hour, we had instructions to meet her the next evening in the Power & Light District, the premier dining and entertainment area in Kansas City. Because of the frequent concerts and events held there, it was a great place to disappear into the crowd, which is likely why Bellarose chose it.

Although I advocated for going in with only Nash as backup, Volkov insisted on a full contingent of shifters stationed throughout the area. Because his face was far too recognizable thanks to his role on the Tribunal, Volkov was forced to wait a block away in the surveillance van. Isaac had grudgingly agreed to allow Dez to compel him. He'd argued for voluntarily helping us, but I wasn't ready to trust his intentions yet. Not after the false memory of Gwen in that mask he'd shown me before. Dez had no trouble compelling Isaac, but he sat at a nearby table as an insurance policy.

I lurked in a nearby coffee shop with a clear view of the outdoor seating area Bellarose chose as the drop site. I'd opted for a classic pickpocketing ensemble—slouchy jeans with great pockets and a dark hooded graphic sweatshirt that wouldn't look out of place in a concert crowd but was also completely unremarkable. It also had an oversized pocket on the front that allowed me to have my dagger in hand while still keeping it out of view. I'd tucked my pink hair beneath a snug-fitting beanie.

After the second cup of hot cocoa, I was sugared up and ready to go. When the call came over the comms that

Bellarose was en route, I tossed my cup in the trash and waited for my opportunity. I didn't have to wait long.

Bellarose looked exactly as she had in Isaac's memory, same wild blonde hair and willowy figure. She wore long, blousy sleeves, but a hint of gold was visible when she moved.

"Is everyone in position?" I asked.

Nash's job was to get Isaac to safety the second I had the cuff since we had no idea how Bellarose might react. Dez was close enough that he could compel anyone who tried to interfere. Once everyone responded, I stepped out of the coffee shop and strolled toward the seating area.

Most people assumed that pickpocketing relied on quick hands and nimble feet. The real art was in the approach. I learned young never to look the mark straight in the eye. Instead, I watched her from the corner of my eye, making it appear that my full attention was on the group of boisterous teens nearby.

Because her guard would be up until she had what she came for, I waited until Bellarose picked up the bag that held our decoy crystal before moving in. She was mere feet from Isaac's table when I brushed up against her, the dagger palmed in my hand.

Nothing happened.

I glanced down to see a familiar flash of gold beneath her sleeve. Unlike with Isaac's cuff, my dagger didn't force this one to uncoil. Volkov was watching the scene through a nearby security camera Dez had hacked, and he must have seen me falter because his voice was in my ear. "Walk away, Riley. We'll get it another way."

But I wasn't ready to give up. I tucked the dagger back in my sweatshirt pocket. I faked a stumble, bumping into Bellarose and flailing my arms to regain my balance. "I'm so sorry," I muttered, grabbing her shoulders to keep her upright. I kept my left hand on her shoulder while my right slipped beneath her sleeve. Despite the cuff I could see on her wrist, my fingers brushed against bare skin. Bellarose smiled and lifted her gaze to mine, and then I saw it. Her features flickered like static on an old television. I dropped my hand and spun around.

We weren't the only ones who came with a decoy. She'd used a distortion spell to make whoever this was into her doppelgänger. The real Zara Bellarose stood across the courtyard, sandwiched between two men who looked like bodyguards but moved like mercenaries as they hustled her into a waiting car and drove away. The only saving grace was that Helen had embedded a failsafe—a tracking spell along with the false memory she stored in that crystal. I crossed my fingers and hoped like hell Bellarose waited until she made it home to unlock the memory because if not, finding her again wasn't going to be easy.

CHAPTER 25

Despite knowing that Zara Bellarose was one of the most powerful witches in North America, I had been prepared for everything except her magic. I'd rushed the job, and it cost me the easy retrieval. Now that she knew we were on to her, that artifact would be even harder to steal. This time, we were going to take the time to understand the mark and plan the heist the right way.

For the past three days, everyone had a task list. Now, we were all camped out in the work room of the Stitch Witch putting the pieces of our plan together. Thanks to Volkov's connections, we knew that Bellarose went into lockdown, ghosting her contacts. And thanks to Helen's tracking spell, we knew she was holed up in a Toronto penthouse.

"Can you get us the layout for her building?" I asked Dez who had spent most of our planning session with his nose buried in his laptop.

He continued typing without looking up. "On it."

"What types of security should we expect?" Nash directed the question to Craig, but Volkov answered.

157

"Bellarose lives in a luxury penthouse, so there will be onsite guards, locked elevators and access points, and high-end tech." Volkov paused. "And that's just the building security. Zara Bellarose doesn't go anywhere without a driver and an armed guard."

Dez looked up from his computer. "We need to get you past biometric locks that use facial and voice recognition."

"Do you have a plan for that?" I asked Dez.

Now that we were talking tech geek, Dez's face lit up. "Yeah. There have been some tech experiences that demonstrated an easy way to fool the facial scan."

I nodded. "Good. I'll let you handle the logistics."

"I'll also need to bring down the firewall from the inside," Dez said, digging in his pocket until he found a thumb drive. "I've got a batch file that will get me in, but I'll need someone to install it."

I nodded like I had a clue what a batch file was. "Noted." I nudged Kali's arm. "You know what that means?"

Volkov and Nash both looked confused. Craig had been around us enough to groan.

Kali rubbed her hands together. "Tell me that you'll need disguises."

"We'll totally need disguises," I agreed.

Nash looked warily at the two of us. "What kind of disguises?"

Kali tapped her finger on her chin. "I'll come up with something."

Bea came in carrying a box of cookies and a liter of pop. When she caught sight of Nash, she tugged her neckline a little lower and winked.

"Behave or get lost," Helen snapped.

"Fine," she agreed, handing out cookies.

Helen snapped her fingers to get everyone's attention. "Don't forget, Bellarose is a powerful witch. She has a particular aptitude for wards and magical warfare."

"Like wands and shit?" Nash asked, earning himself a pinch on the arm from Helen. "What did you do that for?"

"Have some respect," Helen admonished. "This isn't the cartoons. No one uses a wand."

Bea smirked and wiggled her eyebrows. "I use a magic wand."

Dez choked on his cookie.

"Not that kind of wand, you floozy." Helen shoved Bea toward the door. "Go watch the counter."

Bea gave the men a little finger wave but returned to the front of the shop.

Volkov tried to get us back on track. "Helen, what kind of magical warfare should we expect?"

Helen ran through a litany of spells, potions, and magical booby traps Bellarose would have at her disposal.

Nash paled. "Great." He looked over Dez's shoulder, ignoring the huff of annoyance as Dez angled his laptop screen away from Nash. "We need every security feature mapped before we step foot on the property. You sure you're up for that?"

Dez flipped him off. "I'll get tech and security info and the layout," he promised me. "And I'll try to hack into their system to get eyes inside the building. But I won't be able to tell you much about the magical security from behind a screen."

"We need a way to map the interior, including the location of wards and any magical booby traps Bellarose has set." I turned to the group at large. "Any ideas?"

"It's a little unorthodox, but I came up with a plan for that." Dez jumped to his feet and grabbed a medium-sized cardboard box. "I did a deep dive into Bellarose and discovered she has a fear we can exploit."

Volkov and Nash both leaned in.

"What's her fear?" I asked.

Dez reached into the box and pulled out a realistic-looking rubber frog. "She's terrified of frogs. These did not come cheap, but—" He handed the frog to me before passing the box around.

Nash reached in and grabbed an identical frog.

"Um, how many of these tree frogs did you buy, Dez?" I asked, examining the frog. "And what are we supposed to do with them?"

"They had a bulk sale." Dez sounded far too excited about bulk buying. He grabbed the frog out of my hands and flipped it over. "It's retrofitted with sensors and micro cameras. It's also waterproof, can withstand temperatures hot enough to cook Sunday dinner, and has sticky feet" He sat it on the ground with a controller. After pushing a button, the frog hopped across the floor to land on a nearby wall, those sticky feet holding it in place.

"It looks just like a real frog," Helen marveled.

"That's the idea," Dez said. "Think of this guy like an anemometer."

I scrunched my nose. "A what?" I loved Dez, but when he got his nerd on, I had no idea what he was talking about.

"Meteorologists use anemometers to measure wind speed and pressure," Nash explained.

Dez whipped his head around to stare at Nash. "That's correct."

"And you didn't even need to use little words," Nash taunted.

Dez continued as if he hadn't spoken. "Storm chasers also

put anemometers in the path of tornadoes. Once a tornado picks one up, it'll capture all kinds of useful measurements."

"I see where you're going with this." Nash took the controller from Dez and tried it out.

"If we can get a couple of these inside the penthouse," Dez said, "we can map out the security layout." He turned to Helen. "Could you spell these to detect magic?"

"I think we can manage that." She picked up a frog. "We'll test out some ideas and see what we can do."

"How exactly do you plan to get the frogs inside a penthouse?" Nash asked.

Kali and I exchanged a look and grinned. "And we're back to the disguises," I said.

Dez nodded. "I can pose as a delivery person. All I have to do is get Bellarose to take the package inside. I'll put a big enough hole in the box that I can deploy my army of frogs."

Volkov snorted. When I shot him a dirty look, he mouthed, "army of frogs?"

Dez was unperturbed. "And when Bellarose spots one of them, she'll call an exterminator."

Nash looked up from the frog controller. "I'm assuming that's how I get in the penthouse."

Kali tipped her stool over in her excitement. She circled Nash. "I'm thinking a full-on makeover is needed."

Nash backed away. "Hell no."

I pointed at the supernaturals in the room. "Someone has to go in that penthouse to gather intel and install Dez's thumb drive to get past the firewall. You're the only one of us we can be sure that she won't recognize. Plus, you're the one with experience going undercover, right?"

Nash took another step away from Kali, who had grabbed a measuring tape and was attempting to take measurements.

"Stop that," he scolded, playing tug-of-war with the tape. "Why can't I go in like this?"

We all laughed. "No one's letting you in their penthouse looking like that." I gestured to his rumpled clothes and mountain man beard.

Nash didn't look happy about the prospect, but he didn't outright shut it down either.

"Alright. It sounds like we've got a plan. We'll leave tomorrow." I looked at the time. "We need to arrange transportation. Dez and I can get a rental car." I still didn't have a driver's license, or I'd do it myself. "Toronto is a long drive."

Volkov spoke up. "No need. I chartered a plane."

It was presumptuous. Part of me wanted to object, but the rational part of me that didn't want to be trapped in a car with Nash and Dez bickering in the backseat for hours won out. "Great."

"What about the heist? How are you going to steal a cuff that Bellarose will be wearing?" Nash asked.

I grinned. "Leave that part to me."

Everyone stood to leave. Before they could escape, I hopped on top of the table to give my version of a team-rallying speech. After thanking everyone for doing their part, inspiration hit me. What we needed was a team-building experience. Fortunately, I had the perfect activity for it.

"One more thing," I stopped them. "Tonight, we're doing a little team bonding. Meet me at Grinders at 8:00. And Nash? Bring your guitar."

It was karaoke night.

CHAPTER 26

By 8:30, the songs were cued up on the prompter, the lights were dimmed, and the drinks were flowing. The only thing missing was my team.

Kali was the only one who had shown up. She was great company but hated karaoke almost as much as I loved it, so when Craig made an appearance, I let her off the hook and told her to go home. I gave Helen a pass since she needed a full night's sleep before our big trip. I tried—and failed—to not take it personally that Dez, Nash, and Volkov had all ghosted me. In the last thirty minutes, I'd graduated from peppy upbeat tunes to crooning "All By Myself" on stage while staring at the clock above the bar.

I was handing the mic to the next performer when the front door opened, and Dez rushed inside, his red hair standing up like he'd ran his fingers through it countless times. He bypassed the bar to get to me.

"I'm sorry," he said. "I was researching and lost track of time." He looked around the half-empty room, his gaze landing on the table where I'd dropped my jacket and set out a bowl of snack peanuts for all of us. "Where is everyone?"

I shrugged.

Dez's face flushed as he realized he was the only one here. I appreciated the anger on my behalf, but it didn't change the fact that my team building was a giant failure. And if I couldn't count on my team to show up for some drinks and bad songs, could I really get them to pull together on the job? Moping wouldn't change anything though.

I grabbed a handful of peanuts and tugged Dez along with me. Like most nights at Grinders, the owner was working behind the bar. With his towering height and barrel chest, the man certainly lived up to his nickname. Even though most people gave Bear a wide berth, underneath that gruff exterior was a soft and squishy heart. I'd been coming here since I was sixteen years old, and Helen had strong-armed Bear into hosting karaoke night for me.

At the moment, he was watching my approach with his big arms folded over his chest and a bar rag tossed over his shoulder. "Don't even think about it," he grumbled when I moved behind the bar.

"It's free labor, Bear. Take it." I grabbed a glass and reached for the tomato juice and top-shelf vodka.

He took the liquor bottle from my hand and held it out of reach. "I'll make it."

I tried to pull his arm down, but he was immovable. "Don't be like that. Dez likes the way I make it."

Bear snorted. "You mean with actual blood?"

"Exactly." I rooted around in the bar fridge until I came up with the stash of O positive. Most vamps who came in drank it as a straight shot, but Dez needed the mixed drink to get it down. I pressed my hands together like I was praying. "Please, Bear. I've had a shit day."

He cracked. "Fine. But one drink, and then you scoot on the other side of this bar and stay there."

I crossed my heart and snatched the vodka bottle back when he lowered it. I'd made Dez a Bloody Mary so often that I could mix it from memory while listening to him give me the highlight reel of what he found out about Bellarose's tech security features. I grabbed a napkin and set the finished drink on it with a flourish. "So, what you're saying is that beyond the basics, we won't know anything until we're on site?"

"Pretty much," he admitted. To keep our conversation private, we were leaning across the bar with our heads bent together. That's why I didn't see Volkov until he was standing next to Dez.

"Look who decided to show up forty-five minutes late." I tried, and failed, to keep the hurt out of my voice.

Dez lifted the cocktail to his lips and took a long pull, turning sideways on his stool to look anywhere but at us. I put the bottle back on the shelf and stepped out from behind the bar to head back to our table.

"I'm sorry. I would've come sooner, but I got held up." Volkov's arctic blue eyes were solemn. At my questioning look, he said, "Pack business." He didn't elaborate, and I didn't ask. Volkov scanned the room. "Where's Nash?"

"No show loser," Dez muttered under his breath.

I kicked his foot, even though he was right. I was still trying to hold this team together despite their marked lack of enthusiasm.

Volkov motioned to Bear who dutifully poured him his regular drink. Bear pushed the double shot of pricey whiskey across the bar to Volkov. I led the way to our table by the stage, ignoring Volkov's grimace at the performer's off-key enthusiasm as he sat down. Normally, I'd take another turn singing myself, but I wasn't in the mood tonight.

After finishing his drink, Volkov looked at me. "I'll clear my schedule. We can leave for Toronto tomorrow afternoon."

"We?" I asked.

Volkov frowned. "Yes. We."

I held up a hand. "Your job is done, Max. You have Isaac, so you have your witch in custody. You can turn him over to the Enclave and get back to pack business."

He yanked my chair around, so we were face-to-face. "You're not going alone."

"You're right." I patted Dez on the arm. "I'm going with Dez and Nash."

At least, I hoped Nash wouldn't be a no show then, too. Dez wisely kept his opinion on the matter to himself. Although both Helen and Kali had offered to tag along, I'd talked them out of it. Their expertise didn't require them to be in the line of fire. Both women could give us their contributions before we ever left Kansas City.

Volkov leaned closer. "I'm going." If the clenched jaw and bulging vein on his forehead were any indication, Volkov wasn't going to back down.

The commotion at the front door saved me from the argument. I perked up. It might be an hour later than I'd said, but Nash wasn't a no show. Based on the unhappy rooster he carried, I was pretty sure I knew why he'd been late.

The singer on stage trailed off as she watched Nash wrestle the bird cage to our table. Everyone else moved out of Nash's path. I jumped to my feet. "You brought Garth." I hadn't expected him to bring a plus one, but given the bird's namesake, I could get behind the choice.

Nash sat the cage on the table, and I bent down to say hello. When I straightened, Nash was still glaring at Garth. Nash finally broke eye contact with the rooster and looked at me.

"Nice of you to finally show." Dez held his glass up in a mock toast before taking a drink.

Nash looked from Volkov's whiskey glass to the tomato concoction in Dez's hand. "Of course, you'd drink something like that."

"It masks the taste of blood," I explained.

"Let me guess, you don't have the stomach for it, so you can't drink from the source?" Nash shook his head.

Dez moved so fast, even Nash jumped when he reappeared within striking distance of his throat. "I'll make an exception for you." He bared his fangs and let red color his vision.

I scrambled to my feet, but Volkov beat me to them. He shoved Dez back into his chair and got in Nash's face. "Stop provoking him, or next time, I'll let him drain you."

I grabbed Volkov's arm, and he let me pull him away. If I was going to salvage what was left of the night, I needed to get the conversation on more neutral ground. "Where's your guitar?" I asked Nash.

Nash grunted. "I don't perform."

I cocked my head to study him. That didn't make sense. The man practically slept with his acoustic guitar. "Why not?"

"Long story." He didn't sit down to tell it. "I just came to bring you your rooster." Nash grabbed a handful of peanuts before pivoting for the door.

I thrust the bird cage toward Dez and jumped up to follow Nash. "Hey! Wait up," I called after him.

He kept walking, and I followed him outside to the parking lot. "Listen kid, I agreed to do the job, not bond over sing-a-longs. I'll do my part, and you'll get me that classified report." Nash stopped running away long enough to meet my eyes. "That's all this is. I'm not looking for friends."

I tamped down my disappointment at being wrong about him. I thought that once Nash had a job—a purpose—he'd step up and be part of this. But no amount of coaxing or bargaining would make a team player out of Nash if he was determined not to be one. He'd do the job we'd agreed to, and then he'd go his own way.

I stopped chasing after him and tried not to take the rejection personally. "Alright."

He opened the door of his truck, but he never made it inside. I didn't spot the dart sticking out of his back until he face-planted onto the pavement.

CHAPTER 27

I was afraid to leave Nash unprotected in the parking lot, so I sent an S.O.S. text to the group chat after scanning the area. I debated whether to call 911 for a human ambulance or call Bennie who routed our calls to supernaturals embedded within emergency services. Even though Nash was human, I dialed Bennie's number and told him what happened. Then I rolled Nash to his side and sat on the cold pavement with his head cradled in my lap until help arrived.

Volkov and Dez got to us first. "You hurt?" Volkov yelled as soon as he spotted us.

"No." I held up the dart I'd removed from Nash's back. "But someone shot Nash with this. I didn't see who did it."

Once he was assured I wasn't injured, Volkov ran past us to track the shooter.

Dez knelt beside us, all hint of the earlier animosity gone as he checked Nash's vitals. Nash didn't stir even when Dez shined the flashlight app on his phone directly into his eyes.

"His pulse is a bit elevated, which is to be expected, but he's unresponsive. How long has he been like this?"

"A couple minutes. He went down as soon as he was hit. Would a tranquilizer dart do that?" I asked hopefully.

Dez took the dart from my hand, examining the residue on the tip. "Riley, I don't think this is an ordinary tranquilizer."

Volkov came back as an ambulance was pulling into the lot. "Shifter," he growled. "The same one who shot me."

I swallowed past the fear clogging my throat. *It had to be one of Carl's guys. Was he aiming for me and hit Nash by accident? Was this an attempt to take me to Carl?*

I brushed the hair back from Nash's forehead. Without his trademark scowl, he seemed younger and far more vulnerable. Volkov and I were shifters who could heal most injuries. As a vampire, Dez was practically indestructible. Even Helen and the girls had magic at their fingertips. But Nash was human, and I'd brought him into this.

I closed my eyes and bargained with the universe.

Volkov pulled me aside as the paramedics examined Nash. One was a gruff shifter I'd seen at the bar with Volkov. The other was a young witch with healing ability. Neither of them balked at treating a human.

Volkov rubbed the chill from my arms. "They're going to take good care of him."

The young witch approached us. "Alpha," she greeted Volkov before addressing me. "May I see the dart?"

I handed it to her, careful to keep the tip from touching either of our skin. She held it while reciting a reveal incantation. The metal dart glowed in her hand. "As I suspected, this has been coated with some kind of magic." She examined it more closely. "I don't recognize it though. I can send it to the coven elders to see if they can identify the magic," she offered.

Volkov reached for the dart. "That won't be necessary. I'll handle it."

The woman didn't object. "And the human? He's stable for now, but a hospital won't be able to help him."

Volkov didn't hesitate. "Take him to my house." Not surprisingly, he didn't have to give them directions. While they loaded Nash into the ambulance, Dez went back for the rooster, and I called in the calvary, hoping it would be enough to save Nash.

Two hours later, Helen and Bea identified the magic. My stomach pitched at the grim expressions on both their faces.

Bea wrapped an arm around my shoulders and guided me to one of the leather couches in Volkov's library. "You're gonna want to sit for this, sugar." She sank to the seat beside me.

Beneath all the innuendo and makeup, Bea was a care-taker. She was the one who brushed away my tears over a teenage heartbreak and the one who made sure I ate enough when I slid back into the grief of losing my parents. From the way she clutched my arm, whatever they found was bad.

Helen delivered the news. "It's a slow acting magical poison. It causes an immediate paralysis, followed by a gradual deterioration of the vital organs until they fail."

Bea squeezed. "I'm so sorry."

"That's not all," Helen said. "I recognized the smell of that poison as soon as you handed me the dart." She grimaced. "It was the same smell on my cardigan after someone knocked me over at City Market."

The news hit like a blow to the chest. First Helen, then

Volkov with that silver bullet, and now Nash with a poisoned dart. "This is my fault," I whispered.

"Riley, no," Bea said. "None of this is your fault."

But it was. Carl had warned me that if I didn't hand over the Alatyr stone, he'd make me wish I had. I'd been so sure Creed would take Carl out that I had let my guard down, and the people around me paid the price. He was attacking the people I cared about to punish me.

Helen was the smartest witch I knew. If anyone could brew an antidote in time to save Nash, it was her. "But you can fix it, right? Now that you know what it is."

Helen wouldn't look me in the eye. "No. I'm sorry, but there's no known cure. No one has ever lived once the poison is in their system."

I dropped my head to my hands as her words sank in. *No cure.* Nash was going to die, and there was nothing any of my witches could do about it. "How long does he have?" My voice wobbled.

"We don't know for sure," Bea whispered. "There aren't many records of the poison because it requires a great deal of magic and several rare ingredients. And all the known cases were supernaturals."

"What's your best guess?" Volkov asked.

"A few days," Helen answered.

Volkov crouched down next to me, taking my hands in his. "I'll call in some favors with the Witches' Council. If an antidote exists, I'll get it." The council was the international governing body for all witches. If there was a cure, they'd have it. But based on the thinning of Helen's lips, the odds were low.

"It's worth a try," Helen said. "We'll try some spells to see if we can put him into stasis, which might buy us a few more days. But I don't want you to get your hopes up, hon. Barring some kind of miracle cure, he's not going to make it."

Miracles were like wishes, and I'd never reached for them. But for Nash, I would try anything—even if it meant walking straight into hell to get it. "What about a relic?"

Volkov released my hands and stood as he considered it. "It's possible."

While he moved to the bookcase to search, Helen's shoulders drooped. "Oh, hon. I don't know."

Volkov slid the book he had pulled back into place and turned to me with a frown. "You already have something in mind."

I met Helen's worried eyes. "The Alatyr Stone is rumored to be able to heal any injury, rendering the person who holds it virtually indestructible." Maybe that stone would actually be useful for something other than tethering me to Carl.

Volkov nodded. "That's the legend. But no one knows where it is."

I took a deep breath. It was time to face my demons. "I do."

CHAPTER 28

"Let me get this straight." Volkov threw back a shot of whiskey like he'd need it to finish this conversation. "You stole a priceless artifact from Damien Creed's house for Carl and instead of handing it over or selling it, you hid it in Carl's fucking pawnshop."

"Yeah." Years later, and I still got a little rush every time I thought of it right under his nose.

Helen high-fived me, which did nothing to lessen Volkov's anger. He clenched his fist, shattering the glass he still held. He'd ditched the suit jacket as soon as we got to his house, and the rolled sleeves of his dress shirt were stark white against the blood dripping from his clenched fist. Bea fussed over his hand, pressing a tissue against a cut on his palm.

"It's fine."

He tried to brush her off, but she wasn't having it. She swatted his shoulder and continued playing nurse.

"Why would you do something so reckless?" Volkov asked.

It was a fair question. Even at sixteen, I could have sold that chip of the Alatyr stone for enough money to set me up for life. But some things were worth more than money. Restoring my dignity was among them.

I gave Volkov the truth. "Because every day I lived with Carl, he made me feel helpless."

Volkov stared at me so long that the silence grew uncomfortable. Finally, he took the bloodied tissue from Bea and tossed it in the trash. He moved closer and let me see the wolf rising in his eyes. I didn't back away.

"You took your power back." He spoke as if he understood what that felt like.

A conversation for another day. I nodded.

Volkov bent over and began picking up the broken glass, stacking it in a pile on top of his desk. When he finished, he met my eyes. I could see the battle he waged with himself, the way his pale blue irises transitioned to amber and back again. He was a man used to fixing things. But this? This was something only I could fix.

"When do you leave?" He didn't warn me not to go, and he didn't insist on coming. He held himself taut as a bowstring though, every muscle tense as he waited for the answer.

"In the morning." I'd planned to ask Dez to drive me to Santa Fe, but I changed my mind, the question tumbling from my lips before I could change my mind. "Will you come with me? I could use someone to watch my back."

"Always." He didn't touch me, but the rough timbre of his voice felt like a caress just the same.

After asking Helen for scent-masking spells and potion bombs, I spent the remainder of the evening next to Nash's bed. With nothing to distract me, I sank into memories I'd rather leave in the past—the thin strip of light beneath the closet door when Carl locked me inside, the rumble of my stomach the nights I went to bed hungry, the way a gold ring marked my cheek. Sitting here in the dark, I could admit to myself the bone deep terror I felt when I thought about going back there. And as I watched the shallow rise and fall of Nash's chest, I knew I had to do it, anyway.

———

I'd never realized how intimate the interior of a car could feel until I spent twelve hours cocooned in one with Volkov on the drive to Santa Fe. There was only so much a.m. radio I could take before I cracked. The third time I fiddled with the dial, Volkov caught my hand and shut off the radio.

We were almost to Dodge City before Volkov brought up the topic I'd been dreading. "Tell me about the pack."

I stared out the window, counting the windmills dotting the fields while I decided where to start. "When I moved in with Carl, the first thing I noticed was how everyone in the pack was attuned to him. Everyone looked to him when they entered a room. If he was hungry, the women tripped over themselves to feed him. His excitement over a new mark was contagious. And when Carl was cruel, it spread through the ranks like a cancer." I rested my cheek against the cool glass, watching the mile markers as we sped by them. "Carl was a purist who thought mixed packs were an abomination, so he surrounded himself with the worst of the wolves. I was his only exception because I was useful to him."

Volkov didn't interrupt me to ask questions or rush me when I grew quiet. The more he listened, the easier it became to talk about it. I told him about the jobs Carl sent me on and the million little ways he kept us all under the heel of his boot. Once the valve was open, it all came pouring out. I hadn't even realized I was crying until he pulled off the road to give me his full attention. Instead of feeling embarrassed, my heart felt lighter as we started down the road again.

"What can you tell me about Carl's inner circle—his beta and the other dominant wolves in his pack?" Volkov asked.

I ran through the ranked members first, most of whom were yes men. "Carl's beta, Tony, is the one to watch out for. While Carl is calculating and vicious, Tony is the muscle. He's big." I glanced at Volkov whose broad shoulders and strong arms rivaled Tony's. He caught me staring and smiled, flexing as he shifted gears.

I rolled my eyes, even as I admired the view. "As big as you, anyway, and he uses that size to intimidate everyone else in the pack." I thought of my last run-in with Tony, and I sobered.

"Did that extend to you?" Volkov kept his voice calm, but his grip tightened on the steering wheel.

"Every chance he got. For the most part, Carl kept him in line. He didn't want to risk his meal ticket." Bitterness coated my tongue. "Toward the end though, Tony escalated."

"Escalated how?"

"He started watching me all the time, making suggestive comments, brushing up against me, so he could watch me shrink away from him." I battled the embarrassment because I'd be damned if I'd own Tony's shame.

The steering wheel cracked under the strain of Volkov's grip. "You were a child."

"He didn't care."

"Did he touch you?" Volkov's voice was gentle.

"No. I ran before it escalated to that point. But if I had stayed—" I let the thought hang there unfinished.

Unwilling to dwell on it, I spent the next hour running through every dominant wolf in Carl's pack. I'd spent four years cataloging their strengths and weaknesses, and I shared all of it with Volkov.

When we crossed into New Mexico, he knew the pack about as well as I did. Hopefully, we'd be in and out of Santa Fe without Carl knowing we'd ever been there. But I wanted to arm Volkov with as much information as possible. If Carl caught wind of another alpha encroaching on his territory, he'd take it as an act of war.

CHAPTER 29

$\mathcal{I}$t had been dark when we checked into a cheap motel on the outskirts of Santa Fe last night, so it wasn't until this morning that the sights of home rattled my chest and settled into my bones. From my first glimpse of the Sangre de Cristo mountains to the familiar adobe neighborhoods we drove through, I felt nostalgia and grief rise up in equal measure.

Volkov parked in front of a busy café down the street from Carl's pawnshop. Unlike the movies, sitting inside a parked car was a surefire way to get people talking, which is why we were going inside for breakfast. Volkov and I had traded his flashy Audi for a nondescript rental this morning, and we'd doused both the car and our clothes with Helen's scent-blocking potion.

Because there hadn't been time for Helen to concoct a disguise spell, we had to settle for thrift-store disguises. I wore a bland maxi dress that covered my tattoos. A silver and turquoise pendant and the dagger strapped to my thigh were my only accessories. Thanks to Kali's stock of high-end wigs,

179

my hair was long, dark, and braided down my back. Between the wig and the dark contacts, there was nothing distinctive about me.

I'd picked the outfits, so Volkov was stuck wearing a western shirt, bedazzled jeans, and a second-hand rodeo buckle. Even dressed like a dime store cowboy, the man was a smoke show. He didn't exactly blend in, no matter how I dressed him. The best I could do was shove a battered cowboy hat on his head and tell him to try to look timid. I hustled him inside the café before any of Carl's men noticed him.

Because the café was owned by witches, none of Carl's wolves were welcome inside, which made it the perfect surveillance spot. We chose a window table, and Volkov spent the next half hour watching with amusement as I attempted to eat my bodyweight in eggs smothered in green chilies. I may have been gone almost a decade, but Hatch green chilies still tasted like home. If Carl killed me later, at least I'd go out with my belly full and happy.

Volkov took one bite of the spicy chorizo before adding his burrito to my plate. One of the perks of being a goat shifter was a hyperactive metabolism, so I ate it, too. Once I polished off the food, I waved our waitress over.

"Can we get coffee?" It was a good excuse to sit here longer.

"She'll have decaf," Volkov told the waitress.

The idea of me caffeinated must have been frightening enough to warrant putting alpha command behind it. I bit my lip remembering the last time he'd seen me post-caffeine and didn't contradict him. Besides, my nerves were jittery enough. I didn't need to compound them.

As I sipped my drink, I watched the mid-morning shoppers coming and going. I scanned the street again, searching for familiar faces—thankful I didn't see any. The few who ventured into Carl's shop didn't stay long. El Lobo Pawnshop was as rundown as I remembered it. But Carl didn't care about foot traffic. He made his money on the magical contraband he fenced. The rest was just window dressing.

Carl had stepped up his security since I'd left town, and even though it would make stealing the artifact harder, I felt a surge of satisfaction that I'd been the one to wreck his overinflated sense of invincibility. On an earlier drive by, I noted he now had functional security cameras aimed at the front and back exits. According to our chatty waitress, one of the local businesses generously provided private security guards who made the rounds several times each night. From her description of the guards, I was betting those were Carl's guys, and there was nothing altruistic about it.

Volkov waited until the waitress was out of earshot. "How long do you need once you're inside? Two guards would be easy to take out."

For him, it probably would be. "Five minutes, more than likely. Fifteen to be safe." I doubted Carl upgraded the subpar locks on his display cases, but I had to allow for it. "Taking out the guards is too risky though. Even if they don't report in regularly, I know Carl. He'll have tracking apps on all their phones. If one of them goes stationary, he'll know."

Volkov frowned. "What do you suggest?"

"See the store next to the pawnshop?"

He didn't turn his head to look. "The payday loan place or the pet store?"

"The pet store. It's Friday, which means it'll get busy by mid-afternoon. It's also in the same building." I drained the last of my coffee and stole another glance at the businesses across the street. "Even better, it shares a utility room with the pawnshop. Each business has access through a locked door. We could break in after the pet store closes, but we'd risk drawing attention. But during the day, we can walk right in while the pet store is busy. All we need to do is slip inside the utility room and wait for Carl's goons to leave for the night. Once we have the stone, we'll waltz right out the pet store's backdoor."

The only security camera I saw in the alley was the one above the pawnshop exit. Even if there was a camera behind the pet shot, disabling it would be child's play. Although I could take out Carl's cameras just as easy, the less tinkering we did with his security, the less risk he'd notice the tampering.

"Smart." Volkov dropped cash on the table and stood. "We should leave before we draw attention."

I followed him out the door, not breathing normally until we were both inside the rental car.

He checked his watch. "Looks like we've got a few hours to kill.

"Perfect. There's some place I've waited a decade to visit." Fortunately, it was one place in Santa Fe that I was positive none of Carl's minions would step foot inside. I gave him the address of my mother's old studio and mentally prepared myself to be in a space again that meant so much to her.

I took out my contacts and stashed my wig in the backseat for later. On the drive, I told Volkov about my mother, about her talent and the beautiful jewelry she created.

He glanced down as I twisted the ring on my finger. "Did she give you that as a child?" he asked.

"No. I took it from Carl." He'd kept it under glass to remind me of who had all the power, so I stole it from the case before I left for Kansas City. I ran my fingers across the delicate jewel flowers etched into the ring. "It's like a piece of her is forged into the metal. I couldn't leave it behind."

Volkov swallowed. "I understand. When my younger sister Anya died, I kept something of hers." He kept his eyes on the road. "I can barely look at it, but I couldn't let it go."

"The locket?" I guessed. Ever since I stumbled across it in his desk drawer, I'd wondered about the woman who had worn it. When he'd caught me with it, his immediate reaction had been anger. He'd looked at it like that locket was precious. I assumed it was a gift for a woman in his life or maybe a family heirloom or a keepsake from a first love. The truth of it was much worse.

"I'm so sorry you lost her."

"I gave that locket to Anya for her eighth birthday." Sorrow was thick in his voice. "She was ten when she was killed. She died with the locket clutched in her hand like it could save her." He paused as if he wanted to end the story there, but he forced the rest out, each word rawer than the last. "My father made a lot of enemies. The men who gunned Anya down hadn't made a secret of their vendetta, but he was too preoccupied with his women and his vices to take care of it. What kind of alpha can't protect his own daughter from a bullet meant for him? He should have been the one to die, but instead my brother Aleksei and I had to lower the casket with her small body into the ground."

There were no words of comfort that could touch a loss so deep, so I didn't offer any. I reached for his hand, laced our fingers together, and sat with him in his grief. When we arrived, Volkov was in control of his emotions again. We walked up the sidewalk in silence, my heart beating faster with every step.

I hadn't been back here since my mother died. Carl made

sure I had no contact with anyone from my former life after I went to live with him, including the owner of this place. The building was half gallery, half studio space, and my mother spent countless hours here bent over her latest creations. Her jewelry was exquisitely crafted, but sales were rare. Whatever money she made on her art was split between the studio rental and materials.

The building was exactly as I remembered it—cheery and welcoming and so very Santa Fe that it made my heart ache. Before going in, I pressed my palm to the wall beneath the window display to feel the adobe soaking up the morning sun, and I gathered my courage. Then I stepped inside.

The woman who greeted us was more than a decade older, but still dressed in sunset colors, her dark hair curling wildly around her shoulders. Maria Bacca was as vibrant as the last day I saw her. Back then, I'd been a gangly twelve-year-old with dishwater blonde hair and knobby knees, and yet she recognized me the second she spotted me.

Her big brown eyes filled with tears, and she rushed me with both arms open. "Oh my sweet girl, it's been too long. I wondered if you would ever come."

After a few minutes catching up, Maria leaned forward in her chair and grasped my hands. "Your mother left something behind for you. She was making a ring before she was killed in that fire. I saved it all of this time because it was important to her that you have it."

I couldn't force words past the tightness in my throat. All I could do was nod. I followed Maria to the back of the studio where a row of metal lockers held the resident artists' supplies and works-in-progress. When I saw my mother's name— Amelia Cruz—still on the top right locker, all my unanswered questions bubbled up.

I still didn't know why there were no records of my parents or me. And I needed to know why. Although I knew we weren't the only goat shifters on the planet, I'd never met another. Had they had a falling out with their families? Had they been running from something? Were they in some sort of witness protection program? So many questions swirled in my head, and I had to temper the hope rising in me that Maria might be able to give me answers.

"Maria, how long did you know my mother?"

Her smile was soft and full of good memories. "I've known Amelia since she and that handsome husband of hers moved to Santa Fe when you were in diapers."

"Did she ever tell you why she moved here?" I asked, holding my breath for a nugget of information that could help us figure out who she was beyond being my mother.

"She always said she moved here for a new start and stayed for the sunsets."

"Do you know where she lived before coming here?" I asked.

Maria shook her head. "She never said." She sighed. "To be honest, I always got the impression that your parents wanted to put their past behind them. She never wanted to talk about it, and I didn't pry."

I couldn't hide my disappointment. "Did she ever tell you her maiden name, or another name she went by?" When Dez had dug into their past for me, there had been no records for Amelia or Santiago Cruz. But maybe if I had her maiden name, he could track down her earlier records, and we could piece together her life.

"No. I'm sorry." Maria braced her hands on my shoulders and looked into my eyes. "Whatever brought her here doesn't matter. Your mother was a good woman—kind-hearted, funny, and so very smart. And you and your dad were the center of her universe."

I gave her a quick hug. "Thank you."

"Now then." Maria turned the lock combination from memory and reached inside. She pulled out a small box with a stunning silver and copper ring nested inside. "She made this for you."

I lifted the ring out with trembling fingers. The design was different than any of her other creations. Unlike the delicate jewel flowers that were her signature design, this ring was larger, with inlaid copper that looked like some kind of ancient rune. *Why this design?* I ran the pad of my finger over it, marveling at the craftsmanship. It must have taken her hours of work to make it.

Maria wrapped her arm around my shoulder and looked down at the ring in my hands. "It was her finest work, and she made it for you." She pointed to the inscription surrounded by decorative scrollwork that circled the inside of the ring— Daughter of My Heart. Maria patted my arm. "I'll get you a box, so you can take the rest of her belongings."

Volkov packed the contents of the locker for me, while I threaded the ring onto my finger and said goodbye. While I would have loved to linger, Nash was back in Kansas City with magical poison coursing through his veins. When this was all over, I could come back, take Maria out for coffee, and reminisce about the love we shared for my mother. But right now, I had a life to save and a job to finish. I forced myself to walk away.

CHAPTER 30

A few hours later, both Volkov and I had swapped clothes—standard blue jeans and baseball cap for him, loose-fitting yoga pants and sweatshirt for me. After we parked around the corner, we both silenced our phones. Then we packed our pockets full of Helen's potion bombs and waited for a surge of customers to hide us as we slipped inside.

Because two people slinking into the utility room was more likely to be noticed, we decided to split up and go one at a time. Since I was the one with the lock-picking kit, I was going first. I took my time, pausing when I reached the back of the store to make sure no one was watching. Volkov stood in the cat food aisle. I'd lay money on it being the first time he held a catnip toy in his hand. I fought the urge to smile when he lifted his gaze to mine.

A quick scan of the store showed everyone preoccupied with their shopping. But before I could head back, I recognized the man at the counter. That short dark hair, peppered with gray, and wiry build were as familiar to me as Carl's. He was buying the kind of dog treats that were easy to put tranquilizers in. It was one of Carl's go-to tactics to get past guard dogs on a job.

I fought the tremor that shook me at seeing him again. I froze. My vision tunneled until he was all I could see. The last time I'd seen Silas was the night I double-crossed the pack. Carl had sent Silas on the job with me, armed with a bullet meant for me. It was Carl's version of an insurance policy.

I dug my nails into my palm, the bite enough to halt the panic rising in my chest. I should be thankful it was Silas. Any of the other wolves would stand a better chance of detecting our scents if our masking spell failed. Silas was the only werewolf I knew who had lost the ability to shift. He'd been smart enough to hide the defect from Carl. Unless something changed in the years I'd been away, his nose would be no better than that of an average human. Of course, it wouldn't take enhanced eyesight to recognize Volkov if Carl had shown the pack his picture.

I ducked and caught Volkov's attention, willing him to look harmless. Nash's hand signals suddenly seemed like a great idea. Had I been smart enough to teach Volkov what they meant, I wouldn't be crouched down next to the fish food slashing my finger across my throat while pointing to Silas.

Luckily, my charade game was good enough that Volkov picked up on my meaning. Other than a slight jerk of his head toward the back room, he didn't react. When a woman passed me in the aisle, I straightened and sighed like choosing between the varieties of fish food was difficult. She moved on.

Not wanting to risk someone else noticing me, I stepped beyond the aquariums and cat trees, trying to look as if I were searching for the bathroom. The second I was out of sight, I picked up my pace. As I expected, the door to the utility room was locked. In a matter of seconds, I had it open. Rather than relaxing once I made it inside the small room, my fear spiked. The rattle of the furnace kicking on startled me, and I had to force myself not to bolt. Thanks to Carl, I still hated being in dark confined spaces, despite working hard to get past it.

Volkov didn't keep me waiting long. For a large man, he'd mastered moving silently. I didn't hear him approach, the light from the open door alerting me to his presence. He held his finger to his lips, and he reached in his pocket for the dampening bomb Helen sent with us. She'd warned us that it would only mute sound for about an hour. Still, that would buy us enough time for Carl to lock up the pawnshop. Volkov tossed the spelled bomb to the ground and busted it open with his heel. Then he closed the door behind him and locked us in the dark.

I leaned against the wall and slid down, pulling my knees to my chest and wrapping my arms around me. Thanks to my better-than-average night vision, I could make out Volkov's body as he lowered himself to the floor across from me. We stayed like that for several minutes, until my heart rate settled, and the silence became unbearable.

He was the first to break it. "That man at the counter is part of Carl's pack?"

"Yes. His name is Silas." Since I'd already told him about all the dominant wolves in the pack, I didn't need to elaborate. I stretched my legs out and rolled my ankles to keep them loose. I might need to run before this night was over, and I couldn't afford them stiffening up. "How much longer?" I asked when Volkov hit the button to light up his watch.

"Forty-five minutes."

I closed my eyes with a groan. *How could it have only been fifteen minutes?* There was no way I could stand another forty-five minutes stuck in here. I felt this room like a weight on my chest.

"Tell me what's wrong." Volkov demanded. "Was it Silas?"

"No." Out of all Carl's wolves, Silas was probably the least dangerous to me because I knew his secret. "It's this room." He didn't push, but I told him because talking gave me something else to focus on. "Carl used to lock me in the closet to punish me when I did anything he didn't like. He'd leave me in there for hours—no food or water or bathroom breaks. After the first few times, he started duct-taping the cracks, so no flicker of light could make it inside. It took me years to be able to ride in an elevator without panicking," I confessed. "I thought I'd moved past it, but here I am acting like a child scared of the monsters that live in the dark."

"Some things are harder to move past than others." I felt the warmth of Volkov's hand as it circled my ankle, his thumb stroking my skin. "Sometimes you have to replace the bad memories with something better."

Easier said than done.

He pulled off one of my shoes and set it aside, followed by the other shoe and my socks. Then his strong hands were pressing against my arches, his thumbs working magic until I found myself relaxing into his touch.

"Watch your head." It was the only warning he gave me before he grasped both ankles and pulled me closer. "Lean back."

I hesitated for a second before doing as he asked. I closed my eyes, concentrating all of my attention on the feel of his hands against my bare skin.

When all the tension left my body, he reached for my yoga pants, dragging them down my legs and tossing them aside.

His hands trailed up my thighs, snagging my panties next. *Why couldn't I be wearing a sexy thong?* Instead, I'd dressed for practicality. Granny panties might be ugly as sin, but they didn't creep up during a heist.

I caught his hands. "What are you doing?" My voice came out breathless.

Even in the dark, I caught a flash of molten amber as he watched me. "Chasing away your monsters."

I lifted my hips and let go of his hands.

He didn't rush, the anticipation making me burn hotter. By the time he lowered his head, my thighs were trembling. The growl that rumbled against my core was enough to send shockwaves through me. He didn't stop, bringing me to the edge again and again, until the only thing I saw in the darkness was him.

CHAPTER 31

Orgasms were great stress relievers, so much so, in fact, that I waited an extra fifteen minutes until I could be sure my legs would support me. On the plus side, the buffer ensured that the pawnshop was deserted when we made it inside.

From the crowded display shelves to the layer of dust that clung to everything but the gun collection, the place was like stepping into an episode of *Hoarders*. It had always been bad, but it had gone downhill since I quit working here. I could tell it made Volkov's skin crawl. This was a world apart from his family's luxury apartment in Bucharest or his sprawling home outside Kansas City. Volkov did his best not to touch anything.

Volkov looked around the room in disgust. "Now that I've seen this place, I can understand how you could hide an artifact in here that would never be found."

"Have you even been in a pawnshop before?" I asked.

"Yes. I've been in a pawnshop." He checked to make sure the front door was locked and the bathroom empty.

I wasn't sure I believed him. "To buy something?"

He stopped beside me. "Of course not. I had to question the owner about a stolen grimoire."

I tried—and failed—to hide my smirk as I rolled the office chair under the display case on the wall.

Volkov looked at it incredulously. "You put it in the display case?"

"You bet I did." I locked the wheel and climbed on the chair, picking the lock with ease. The stone was right where I left it, stuffed inside a boxing glove.

Because the stone was a chip from a larger rock, its edges were jagged against my palm. It was a stunning white with flecks of amber that rivaled Volkov's eyes, and the stone had delicate symbols etched into its surface. When I'd stolen it, I was skeptical that it had any sort of magical powers, much less the ability to grant someone near immortality. I closed my fist around it and waited for a magical charge to reassure me that this would work, but it felt like any other stone in my hand. I tucked it into my sweatshirt pocket, hoping for Nash's sake that it was real.

I relocked the display case and put the chair back where I found it. Volkov tensed and put his body between me and the door before I heard the scrape of the key as someone unlocked it. I grabbed a fistful of his shirt and tugged him backward. We had what we came for. If we hurried, we could make it out the back before anyone spotted us.

The slow clap stopped me. "Bravo, kid. All this time searching, and it was here the whole time." I didn't have to see him to recognize Carl's voice. It had echoed in my nightmares for years.

Tony and two other wolves came in through the front. I took my hand out of my pocket and turned to face him, not wanting Carl at my back no matter how many of his wolves followed Tony in.

"I don't know what you're talking about," I said, pressing my back against Volkov's as he snarled a warning at the others.

Carl's lips twisted in a cruel smile. "Don't play dumb with me, girl." He pointed to a shelf that held collectibles, the flashing light of the camera only visible when I looked directly at it. "I've been watching since you stepped foot in here."

A shiver of unease ran down my spine. We'd only been in the pawnshop for minutes, not nearly enough time for Carl and his goons to get here from the house. "You knew we were coming," I accused. "How?" I mentally ran through the list of everyone who knew we were headed here, wondering who could have sold us out. Isaac? Teagan? There was no one else I'd even entertain as a possibility.

Carl prowled closer, momentarily stopping when Volkov turned sideways so he could keep everyone in his sights, moving me along with him, so we still stood back to back. Now that I had a full view of the room, I could see just how screwed we were. Beyond Tony and the two wolves who had followed him inside, I counted at least six through the window waiting out front. There were probably just as many waiting out back for us should we make it that far.

Carl savored my fear until I got it under control again.

"I had a tail on you for months," Carl said.

If he'd had someone following me for months, why the sudden escalation? His threats started long before I tipped Creed off to his double-cross. "Do you have a buyer lined up?" I saw I hit a nerve. "Let me guess. Zara Bellarose?"

Carl stiffened. "I wasn't about to let her get to you and take my stone. I've been looking for the Alatyr stone for too long to let it go."

He was never going to hand it over. There's no one he wouldn't sell out. First, Creed. And he would have done the same to Bellarose. "So, what? She contacted you about it, and you decided to come after me?"

"When my guys couldn't find the stone and the threats didn't get you to hand it over, I decided to give you a little incentive to go get it." He smiled.

When his meaning sunk in, I lunged for Carl, but Volkov grabbed my arm and yanked me back. "Don't play into his hand," Volkov warned. I stopped because he was right. Like it or not, Carl was bigger and stronger than I was. I couldn't afford to be reckless.

"The shifter was yours. You went after Helen. Then you had Max shot with silver, and when he healed, you sent your man after Nash. Slow-acting poison to give me time to go after the stone."

"You always were a smart kid," Carl said. "Just not smart enough to see the trap coming." He walked over to the weapons case, choosing a wicked-looking Bowie knife before turning back to me. "Remember when I told you about what happened to the last guy dumb enough to cross me?" He kissed the blade like a total freak. "Carved him up like a Thanksgiving turkey and left the pieces for his kids to find."

"You're sick, you know that?"

He held out his hand. "Give me the stone, and I'll make your death easy for old time's sake."

I stepped away from Volkov, settling my weight on the ball of my foot and bending my knees. "That's not going to happen." I came here for the stone, and I was determined to walk out of here with it. I'd be damned if I handed it over without a fight.

"Stop!" Volkov put every bit of his alpha power behind the command. "No one touches her."

I elbowed him in the back. "Or you," I added.

He grunted but didn't amend the order.

Carl staggered. There was no doubt who was the stronger alpha, and for a second, I thought it might be that easy. But then Carl straightened and tapped his ear. "Noise canceling ear plugs come in handy."

Volkov pressed his back into mine, his voice low. "I don't suppose you'll run if I give you an opening?"

"Not a chance. We're in this together."

Volkov sucked in a deep breath, letting it out slowly. He patted my side, where I'd strapped on the sheath holding my demon blade. "Then make it hurt."

I squeezed his hand before taking a step away.

"Which one of you is Tony?" Volkov called, even though from the description I gave him, I was sure he already knew. "Because I'm going to rip your throat out last, so I can take my time."

I pulled my dagger as Volkov launched himself at the trio of men, ripping through his clothes and shifting into his massive black wolf mid-air. His wolf was as savage as he was beautiful, but the fight would still be three to one. I resisted the urge to watch, focusing all my attention on the man who had stolen four years of my life.

CHAPTER 32

I tuned out the sound of the fight raging behind me and waited for Carl to make the first move. Unlike a lot of the wolves in his pack, Carl wasn't a brawler. He didn't have the sheer mass of Tony, nor the speed of some of the young wolves. But he could match any of them in brutality when he wanted.

His real advantage though was that Carl fought smart. He took the time to size up his opponents and exploited every weakness he found. So, I gave him one to attack, favoring my right side when he made his move. I swung at him with the dagger in my right hand, kicked with my right foot. Even when I dodged and feinted, I moved to the right.

Carl was toying with me, and we both knew it. I kept dancing out of reach as he tested my defenses. I slowed my reactions enough to make him think I was tired, and I panted like my lungs were on fire. When he was sure he had me on my heels, he struck hard and fast, kicking the dagger from my hand before aiming a strike at the ribs on my left as I'd hoped he would.

I was ready for him. Stepping to the side, I grabbed his arm with my left hand and brought my right elbow down with a crack. His Bowie knife clattered to the floor. I brought the heel of my foot down on his instep and my knee up to meet his face when he doubled over. I'd practiced those moves a hundred times on the mat until I could execute them in my sleep. While he was still reeling from the blow, I grabbed his knife from the floor. Yet, when I brought it up for the killing blow, I hesitated.

"So, you have some fight in you, after all," Carl taunted.

He wiped the blood from his lip. "I wondered after I killed your parents." He smiled and cracked his neck. "You must have known I set that fire, but still you came home with me— did as you were told."

Rationally, I knew I'd been too young at twelve to fight back against a man like Carl, that I hadn't had a choice. The knowledge did nothing to lessen the hole his confession burned in my gut. I felt sick as I looked at him. I'd slept under the roof of my parents' killer for years, ate from his table, stole for him so he could afford all the things my parents never could. The blow was worse than any he could have delivered with his fists.

Carl didn't hesitate. He hooked his foot behind my leg and shoved as he got to his feet, sending me careening into a display case. When he came for me, he didn't hold back. The first blow glanced off my cheek, the second doubled me over, and the third sent me sprawling at his feet.

I scrambled to my knees, barely dodging the boot he aimed for my face.

Carl grabbed a fistful of hair and yanked my head back. He lifted his fist, exposing his middle. A knife to the gut was a good way to incapacitate a werewolf. It might cost me, but I didn't go for the easy strike, Volkov's words ringing in my ears. Instead, I flipped the blade in my hand, so it faced up, and then I drove Carl's own knife straight through his dick. He curled into himself, hands cupped over his crotch as he let loose a high keening scream that hurt my ears.

I faltered for a second, my stomach twisting at the thought of taking another life—no matter how much he deserved it. But then I imagined my mother's beautiful face and my father's kind eyes as they were engulfed in flames from the fire Carl lit. I tossed the Bowie knife aside and picked up the dagger I dropped. I stepped behind him and sliced it across his throat.

I didn't drop his body until I was sure he was dead. Then I clutched the dagger, watching as it soaked up Carl's blood like a delicacy. The demon magic fed on his sacrifice. I don't know how long I stood there watching his body to make sure it didn't twitch back to life.

Strong fingers pried mine loose, taking the dagger from my grip. Volkov set it aside before holding me against his chest. "It's over." He stroked a hand down my hair and pressed his lips to the top of my head. "Let's go home."

Blinking back the tears that threatened to spill, I left the shelter of his arms. I didn't have time to fall apart. I went into the pawnshop's bathroom and stared in the mirror as I washed the blood from my hands.

When I came out, Volkov was dressed again. While I looked like I'd spent the evening moonlighting as a wiffle ball, Volkov looked mildly rumpled wearing his borrowed clothes. He barely had a scratch on him, despite killing three men.

"Are you okay?" I asked, putting my dagger back into its sheath

He looked down at Tony's body with a grim smile. "I am now."

Volkov called the Enclave to report the deaths. Although I was tempted to burn the place to the ground, I left the mess for the cleaning crew they'd send in behind us. I tucked the stone we came here for into my pocket. Hopefully, it would be enough.

When we walked outside, what was left of Carl's pack had scattered, leaving us alone in the alley. The night sky was clear, the full moon guiding the way as I limped toward the car, my body already stiff from the beating I just took. For years, I'd imagined what it would feel like to be free of Carl. I might not have to look over my shoulder anymore, but I'd have to live with the knowledge that I'd spent years with my parents' killer. I thought his death would bring me peace, closure even. But all I felt was numb.

CHAPTER 33

Thanks to Volkov's speeding habit, we made it back to Kansas City an hour after nightfall. I didn't have the strength to go through my mother's belongings yet, so Volkov promised to keep them safe until I was ready. Because there was a brush among her things, he offered to send the hair in it to his contact at the state lab for a DNA analysis that could help identify her real last name. I agreed but didn't get my hopes up.

All four witches were jockeying for position with their faces pressed to the library window when Volkov parked in his driveway. They'd been taking turns watching over Nash when we were gone, but I'd called on the way home, so they knew when to expect us.

Helen met me at the door, a pinched expression on her face. Nash must have taken a turn for the worse. "Did you get it?"

I pulled the Alatyr stone out of my pocket and handed it to her. Alyce, Bea, and Janis crowded around Helen to get a good look.

Helen held the stone reverently. "Do you feel that?" she asked the others.

They all nodded. "Powerful magic," Alyce declared.

I'd always envied how they could sense magic. Hearing them now, hope bloomed in my chest. *This might actually work.* "How do we do this?"

The women frowned down at the stone. "Maybe we should use it like those hot stone massages they do at that fancy spa down the street from the Stitch Witch," Bea suggested.

Helen batted her hand away. "That's ridiculous. You don't use an ancient relic to give a massage." She studied the symbols on it. "We could place it on his chest over his heart."

"Or over the wound," Alyce said.

Janis traced the surface with her finger. "Maybe we should do a healing spell with it."

While the witches continued to bicker about the best way to use the relic, Volkov walked past them into his kitchen, stopping abruptly when he caught sight of the state of it. His normally pristine granite island was covered with casserole dishes, baked goods, and a container of Jell-O with something questionable submerged in it.

Alyce beamed at him. "We thought you might be hungry after your trip, so Helen and I cooked some of our specialties for you."

Volkov opened the lid of the Jell-O tentatively and sniffed, then quickly closed the container again. "How thoughtful." He tried to hide his grimace. "But I don't seem to have an appetite right now." He looked down the hall longingly toward his bedroom.

After the last few days, I didn't blame him for needing some alone time, particularly when faced with four elderly witches who had taken over his home. "Go on. I'll let you know if Nash wakes up."

After he was gone, Helen scanned me from head to toe. "You look like hell, hon."

"I'll tell you all about it tomorrow." I jerked my head toward Nash's room. "But right now, let's go see if we can work a miracle."

Nash looked paler than when I'd left him, and the web of veins across his shoulder and chest were a mottled gray.

"It's the poison. It spreads a little more by the hour." Helen placed the stone in Nash's hand. "I think it would be best if he's touching as much of the surface as possible," she explained, closing his hand in a fist around the stone. She nodded to the others, who began chanting a standard healing spell, their voices mingling like a well-rehearsed choir.

While they worked their healing magic, I pulled a chair next to the bed and sat beside Nash, watching for any sign that the poison was receding. When nothing happened, I felt the hope fade. "Now what?" I asked.

"Now, we wait." Helen patted my shoulder. "Are you staying?"

At my nod, everyone but Helen gave me quick hugs before filing out of the room. It was well after Janis' bedtime, and all of my witches looked like they could use a good night's sleep. Helen offered to bring me some food before she left for the night.

"Anything but Alyce's Franken-Jell-O," I whispered low enough Alyce wouldn't hear me.

She was convinced we all secretly loved it because it was the first thing to disappear at a potluck. The truth was we dumped it down the garbage disposal when she wasn't looking. Helen brought me a plate with a little of everything else, and I picked at the food. Listening to the rasp of Nash's labored breathing killed my appetite, so I set it aside.

"Where's Nash's rooster? With Dez?" I should have texted Dez to check in.

Helen looked down at Nash. "That poor bird put up a big ruckus until Dez brought him over. I think he wanted to stay with Nash."

I looked around the room for the birdcage but didn't see it. Helen crossed the room to the closet doors and opened them. Sure enough, Garth was perched on the highest clothing rod, his little head tucked into his feathers.

"He didn't like being so cooped up," Helen said. She pointed to the floor that was covered with newspapers to catch Garth's nightly deposits.

I covered my mouth to smoother the laugh. Volkov was going to have an absolute meltdown when he found out. The levity felt good after the week I'd had.

Helen closed the doors again, eyes twinkling. "I'll be back to check on you both in the morning." She pointed a bony finger at my chest. "Get some sleep. The magic doesn't work any better when you're watching for it." She squeezed my shoulder on her way out.

Alone with Nash, I wrapped my hand around his to make sure the stone made optimum contact with his skin. Because I'd read somewhere that talking could help unconscious people feel less alone, I talked. I told him about my witches and how I came to live with them, how Craig and Volkov busted me pickpocketing one of their friends, and how I met Dez. Although it was probably my imagination, Nash's color seemed to improve, the gray in his veins starting to tint blue. So, I kept talking.

Sitting here in the quiet of the early morning hours with

exhaustion setting in, I told him about Carl. Nash didn't stir, but I found once I opened the floodgates, it was hard to shut them. If he woke up, he wouldn't remember any of this, anyway, so I didn't hold anything back.

"I'm afraid to go to sleep," I admitted when I could barely keep my eyelids open. "Afraid I'll see him. For years, I imagined killing him for what he'd done—for what he made me do. I thought killing Carl would erase him from my nightmares, but now, I'm afraid it carved out a permanent place for him to live inside me."

I must have fallen asleep in minutes because when I opened my eyes again, sunlight was streaming through the window.

"My throat feels like shit."

I swung my head around. "Nash?"

His face was still pale and his hands shaky, but his hazel eyes were wide open and alert. I dropped my head into my hands and took a deep breath and then another. It had actually worked. That stone really had magic in it. Until he'd opened his eyes, I hadn't dared to believe we'd get a second chance.

"My throat still feels like shit," he rasped. When I looked up, Nash cupped his throat and pointed at the nightstand where Helen had left a glass of water. I tried to help him sit up to drink it, but he pushed my hands away to do it himself. Once he was propped up on a pillow, I handed him the water.

"Slow down," I warned when he guzzled the water.

He took another drink before handing it back to me.

"How do you feel?" I scanned his bare chest, relaxing when I saw the color of his veins was back to normal. Nash must have dropped the stone because it was on the carpet next to the bed. I picked it up and wrapped his hand around it again.

He stared down at it, then at me. "What happened?" As if his memory was stitching back together, he reached a hand behind his shoulder and felt the bandage. "I was shot."

"Poison dart. Can you believe that medieval shit?" I joked.

Nash winced and rotated his stiff shoulder. "Get me up to speed."

"Let's get you comfortable then because it's going to take a while." I grabbed another pillow and stuffed it behind his back, and then I threw my arms around him. Nash froze as I hugged him. As soon as I let go, I grabbed my phone to send a group text. This time, I didn't even hold back on the emojis.

CHAPTER 34

"You're not going. It's too dangerous." I crossed my arms and blocked the doorway, so Nash couldn't get past me. Nash was back to his usual cranky, obstinate self. Except this time, instead of trying to ditch me like he normally did, he insisted on going on this heist despite the fact that he was on death's doorstep a few hours ago.

"You already got shot once because of me, and you almost died." I should never have recruited a human, no matter how tough he seemed. But I could do the right thing now and cut him loose.

Nash mimicked my stance, crossing his arms over his chest. "It's not the first time I got shot." He pointed to a scar on his arm. When I didn't budge from the door, Nash sighed. "It wasn't your fault, Riley."

"My old alpha shot you to get to me. In my book, that makes it a pretty clear-cut case of my fault."

"You are not responsible for what some psycho alpha did. None of it, do you hear me?" Nash picked up the Alatyr stone and held it up. "Besides, you saved my life with this."

I shrugged. I wouldn't have had to save his life if I hadn't pulled him into this mess in the first place. "This kind of work is too dangerous for a human."

"Bullshit," he argued. He put a hand on my shoulder and waited for me to look at him. "I heard you last night, Riley. Taking a life isn't easy. Trust me. I know what it cost you to go back there. But you did it. For me. So, whether you like it or not, I'm going."

I stared at the light fixture until I was sure I wouldn't cry. Then I pointed to the rumpled bed. "You need to rest."

Nash laughed, which quickly turned into a cough, followed by a wheeze. "Who can rest with that demon rooster around?"

"His name is Garth, and he missed you," I said.

He turned and glared at the closet, where Garth was pecking at the door, trying to find a way out. I'd texted Helen to bring the birdcage over when Volkov left for his morning run, but she hadn't arrived yet. I glanced at the clock. If she didn't get here soon, I'd have to sneak Garth out the window before Volkov caught us.

As if she knew I was thinking about her, Helen opened the front door. I called out, so she'd know where we were and moved aside, allowing her and Janis to come into the bedroom. Both witches looked well rested this morning. Janis wore her usual peasant skirt and tunic, her hennaed hair plaited down her back. Helen was wearing her no-nonsense cardigan, with a giant leather glove on one hand and a can of air freshener in the other. Neither of them carried the birdcage.

"I brought you something to eat." Janis sat the breakfast sandwich and large coffee she carried on the nightstand. She stood on her tiptoes and pinched Nash's cheeks. "Looks like you've got some color back. A hearty breakfast, and you'll be as good as new," she declared.

Nash jerked his head toward the door. I pointed at the bed again before looking at Helen. "Where's the cage?"

"It's in the entry, but we don't need it. I have this." Helen waved her gloved hand in the air, and then stepped around me to check on her patient. "Well, look at you! On your feet and everything. While you've been napping, we've been training your pet rooster."

"He's not my pet," Nash grumbled, sitting down on the edge of the bed and picking up his sandwich.

"Psssh," Helen dismissed his objection, walked to the closet, and threw open the doors. "Watch this." She lifted her gloved hand in the air and whistled.

I winced. Helen could out-whistle construction crews, and in a room this size, the sound was far too loud. Garth didn't seem to mind though. He flapped his wings and took off at a run before awkwardly flying toward her knees. Helen crouched down and extended her arm, so Garth could perch on it. Once he was settled, she stood up. "Ta da!"

Nash stared at her and then stuffed the rest of his breakfast sandwich in his mouth, so he didn't have to comment.

"You know that's a chicken, right?" I had to ask. "Not a hawk."

Helen shushed me. "Don't you sass me." She scratched Garth's chest before holding him down for Nash. "Tell your daddy goodbye, Garth."

Nash swallowed too fast, and Janis had to slap him on the back to dislodge it. Garth took one look at Nash's red face, puffed up his chest, and crowed.

"What a good boy," I cooed.

As soon as Garth stopped crowing, I heard the garage door

open. That meant we didn't have a lot of time. I hurried Helen out the door. "Quick. Get him in the cage before Volkov sees him."

She bristled but did as I asked. I rushed over and closed the closet doors before Volkov could see the giant chicken poop tower under Garth's make-shift roost. I grabbed the bottle of air freshener Helen brought to cover our tracks and sprayed the room. Twice.

Nash plugged his nose and backed away. When I heard Volkov's heavy footsteps, I stuffed the air freshener in my waistband and tried to look innocent.

Volkov stopped abruptly when he reached the door. "Why does it smell like a chemical sugar cookie in here?"

I pointed to Nash who had sat back down on the bed. "Nash likes it." I turned so Volkov couldn't see me and widened my eyes at Nash, hoping he'd play along. It was his rooster we were hiding, after all.

Volkov entered the room and stared at Nash. "I'll be damned. It actually worked."

"Why do you sound so surprised?" I asked.

Volkov picked up the stone and examined it. "I thought it was an old wives' tale."

This was the first he voiced any doubt. "You thought it was fake, but you came with me, anyway. Why?"

"Because you asked." He tossed me the stone. "Dez pulled into the driveway in that toy car of his right after I got here."

That was fast. I'd texted Dez as soon as I woke up, but I thought it would take him longer. "Great. I'll grab Helen and Janis and then meet you guys in the library. We've got a heist to pull off." I waited until Volkov was down the hall before putting the air freshener on the nightstand.

Nash grabbed his shirt from a nearby chair and pulled it

over his head, grabbed his coffee, and followed me out. When I tried to object, he planted a hand between my shoulder blades and propelled me out the door.

"I'm coming," he groused. "We're a team, remember?"

"Fine." We could use his input, and it wasn't like he could injure himself in a planning meeting.

Dez and Helen had been busy while we were gone. Dez mapped out all of Zara Bellarose's physical security features. In addition to watching over Nash and teaching Garth some new tricks, Helen brewed up a special stash of potion bombs.

She dumped them out of the paper lunch sack she brought them in and arranged them on Volkov's desk. "I made a few more scent-blockers since I figured you used your stash up. Oh, and another sound dampening spell. Did you use the one I sent with you? It was a new recipe."

Volkov smiled. "Oh, we definitely used it."

I felt my cheeks heat as I remembered the kind of noises it covered. When Volkov's smile widened, I promptly changed the subject. "What's this one do?" I picked up a potion ball that looked almost translucent.

"This little beauty is an incognito spell. It's like your own chameleon suit. It won't make you invisible, but it's the next best thing. It'll help you blend into the surroundings. Unless someone is really looking, they won't see you. It only lasts about twenty minutes though, so don't use it until you need it."

"And these?" Nash pointed to an assortment of sparkly balls.

Helen clapped her hands and cackled. "Those are your attack potions. We've got stun bombs, flash potions, ants-in-your-pants, and the classic glitter bombs.

Nash's eyebrows shot into his hairline. "Glitter bombs?"

He didn't comment on the ants-in-your-pants. That one must be self-explanatory.

"Don't knock them. They pack more of a punch than you'd think." I smirked at Volkov, remembering the last time Dez and I used them to save his ass. It was Volkov's turn to flush.

Helen gathered up the potion balls and put them back in the sack.

"Okay," I said. "We've got the artillery and a run-down of the physical and tech security measures. And Kali will be here this afternoon to drop off disguises." I frowned, trying to figure out how we could get inside without Nash. "Maybe we can find another way to get the frogs inside, so Dez can pose as the exterminator."

Nash looked at Dez, who was nervously bouncing his foot. "No. I'll do it," Nash insisted.

"Eager for your makeover, there, Sasquatch?" Dez teased, a little less animosity in his tone than usual.

I guess Nash's brush with death mellowed the rivalry. "Nash, we've been over this. You need to sit this one out. Bellarose is one of the most dangerous witches in North America. It's just too dangerous for a human."

"About that," Helen said. "I have an idea to make Nash here harder to kill."

"Does it involve a cape?" Dez asked. "Because I'm down for a superhero cape."

Janis giggled, and Helen ignored him. She picked up the Alatyr stone from the desk where I'd put it. "We think we can make this into a talisman. Since it's capable of healing almost any injury, wearing a chip of it should make Nash virtually indestructible."

Nash grinned. "There you have it. Cape or not, I'll practically be a superhero while I wear it."

"How soon can you have it?" I asked.

Helen and Janis bent their heads together to confer. "A couple hours should do it. It's a pretty straight-forward transformation spell, and we have all the ingredients we need at the shop."

Everyone dispersed to get ready for the trip. Dez hung back until we were the only two left in the room. "Can I talk to you?" he asked.

"Of course. What's up?"

"I brought something along that you should see, but I left it in my car."

"Okay." I helped him pack up his spy frogs and followed him outside.

He opened the passenger door for me. He grabbed a manilla file folder from the back before sitting in the driver's seat. "I got the classified report on Nash that you asked for."

"Great! Nash will be glad to get some answers." I reached for it, but Dez held it out of reach.

"I'm not sure now is a good time to give it to him. We're about to go into a situation where everyone needs to be on their A game. And Riley," he handed me the folder. "This is going to mess with his head."

I opened the folder and started reading. My mouth dropped when I saw paragraphs about a recovered demon artifact. Apparently, the Army knew a lot more about supernaturals, or demons at least, than I'd guessed. But that wasn't the worst. The more I read, the more I understood what Dez meant. This report was about Nash as much as it was about the op.

Much like the supernatural governing bodies, the Army had a vamp on retainer to wipe memories. When it didn't work on Nash, the Army had hung him out to dry. Not only did they kill his career, but they also launched a smear campaign that shredded his reputation. They made Nash look like an unhinged conspiracy theorist, so no one would take him seriously when he started talking about demons.

I leaned back in my seat. This report would devastate Nash. To have the organization that he fought and bled for screw him over like that.

Dez let me process it for a couple minutes, then he faced me. "You can't give him this right now."

"He deserves to know."

Dez nodded. "He does. But now isn't the time. Think about how he's going to take this, Riley. Sitting on the info for a few more days won't hurt anything. Once we're done with this job, it won't matter if he falls apart."

He had a point.

CHAPTER 35

olkov drove us to the downtown airport where his chartered plane waited. While everyone else checked out the swanky interior, Volkov grabbed my hand and pulled me aside. Before I could ask any questions, he wrapped one arm around my waist and used the other hand to cradle the back of my head as he lowered his lips to mine. The man kissed like he didn't care who was watching, his tongue teasing mine until my whole body was in tune with his. When he finally lifted his head, I gripped his forearms to hold myself steady.

"Be careful," he said.

I blinked as I tried to make sense of the warning. "You're not going to Toronto?" It was so unexpected, I assumed I misunderstood.

"You said once that this was something you had to do for yourself."

I nodded because it was true.

His arms tensed beneath my hands, and he stared down at

the silver and copper ring on my finger. "I trust you'll call if you need me."

I twined a hand in his dark hair and pulled him down for another kiss. This time, I put everything I had into it, so that he would have no doubt about how I felt. "Thank you," I whispered when we pulled apart. Then I climbed the stairs and joined my team, who had already busted out the snacks.

The flight to Toronto was spent strategizing and laughing with Dez, Nash, and Helen, who had decided to come along for on-the-ground magical support. For the first time since I pulled them together, we felt like a real team. And that made handing over the classified folder in my bag even harder.

Although I'd been tempted to hold on to it until the flight back, I couldn't shake the feeling that doing so would be the first step down a slippery slope. I swore when I stepped back into this world, that I would do things differently. I saw the devastation and division that doing things Carl's way wrought. If I held back this information for the good of the job, how long would it be before it became a habit. There'd always be a way to justify doing the wrong thing. To be in this together, I had to have my teammates' backs and trust them to have mine in return.

I snagged the folder out of my bag, unbuckled, and moved to the seat next to Nash. When he looked up, I handed him the report Dez dug up before I could change my mind.

"What's this?" he asked, looking ten years younger now that Kali had given him a shave and a clean-cut haircut for his disguise. Without all that scruff he hid behind, Nash was a handsome man with striking hazel eyes and great cheekbones. Somehow, seeing him fresh-faced made this even harder.

"It's the classified report from your Peru op." I placed my

hand over the folder, holding its secrets inside for a bit longer. "You're not going to like what you find in here, and I'm sorry for that. But you deserve to know what happened to you."

His jaw hardened as he stared down at it. I removed my hand and left him to read through it without an audience.

After we landed, we checked into a short-term rental a block from Zara Bellarose's penthouse. The place had four bedrooms, a Jacuzzi tub, and a rental fee that gave me sticker shock. But it provided an ideal launchpad for our operation. Besides, I wasn't the one overpaying. It was a business expense.

No matter how I tried to draw him into the planning, Nash answered in monosyllables for the rest of the day. I hoped I hadn't just screwed the job by handing him that report. Everyone else conducted a little recon before calling it a night. Tomorrow would be a big day, and we could use all the rest we could get.

"I'm not coming out." Dez's voice was muffled through the bathroom door.

"It can't be that bad," I coaxed.

Although we weren't going in to steal Valac's cuff until after dark, we needed to get the full layout of the security this morning in order to finalize our plan. That meant Dez was up first. After a lot of discussion, we decided it was probably best not to pose as a major shipping company since we couldn't be sure they wouldn't deliver another package the same day. Instead, Dez poked around in Bellarose's business enough that he came up with an occasional business associate who was fond of using a trendy courier service with an eclectic staff. It was the perfect cover.

Because Kali assured me no one would recognize Dez in this costume even if they had a picture of him in front of them, I hadn't peeked inside the bag before handing it over. *How bad could a courier costume be?* "Dez. We don't have time for this. Stop being a baby."

The door clicked open, and Helen and I craned our necks to get a look as he came out of the bathroom.

"Oh my," Helen whispered.

I was at a temporary loss for words as I checked out Dez. Kali had outdone herself with this one. Instead of going for a generic look, she transformed him into a definitely-make-an-impression kind of guy. It was brilliant, really. Normally, Dez looked like an average computer programmer in his uniform of khakis and button-up shirts, his ginger hair and beard neatly groomed. But this? This was punk rock perfection.

She'd put him in skin-tight leather pants, a Diodes t-shirt that I was seriously impressed she sourced so quickly, and a beat-up leather jacket that rivaled my own. Dez's hair was spiked into a faux hawk, and he had a temporary scrollwork tattoo peeking out of his collar. He wore two small silver hoops that emphasized his full lower lip and a matching bull nose ring through his septum.

I whistled.

He looked down at his outfit and rubbed his nose like it itched. "I look ridiculous."

"Are you kidding me? You look hot as fuck," I assured him.

Kali had been right. Dez was one of my best friends, and I barely recognized him under all that punk rock goodness. If he brought out those fangs of his, women would be practically tossing their panties at him.

I pointed to his nose ring. "Magnetic?"

"Yeah." He shifted his weight self-consciously, drawing attention to those painted-on leather pants.

When he caught Helen staring at his crotch, she grinned. "Well, good for you."

He turned as red as his hair, pivoted, and locked himself in the bathroom. It was probably good that Nash wasn't here to tease him, or I'd never get Dez out again. I just hoped Nash got his head straight before tonight because we were going to need him.

"Come on, Dez. Be a good sport. You'll be in and out in less than an hour, and then you can change your clothes and deploy your frog army." I tried not to snicker at the idea of an army of frogs invading Bellarose's fancy high-rise penthouse.

The promise of using his new tech toys was enough of a carrot to get Dez out of the bathroom. Helen discreetly snapped a photo when he wasn't looking and winked at me.

He grabbed the box with the fake shipping label he'd brought along. He'd added a false bottom to the box for his frogs and cut a trap door in the side that blended in with the logo if you didn't look too closely. He'd tested it earlier, and the frogs had enough power to push it open when the time came. We were banking on Bellarose not being the type to break-down empty boxes for recycling.

He tucked the box under his arm and walked to the door. "Let's get this over with."

"Hold up." I adjusted the tiny camera disguised as one of the metal studs on his jacket and then pushed his shoulders back. "Remember, you have to sell this. The second you walk out that door, you need to be all piss and swagger."

He nodded, then lifted one corner of his mouth into a sneer while managing to look bored.

Who was this man? "That's perfect." I shoved him out the door before he could change his mind.

Half an hour later, the package was on the entry table where Bellarose's maid put it after she signed for it and slipped Dez her phone number. By the time Dez made it back to the rental, Nash had roused himself and joined us.

He took in Dez's outfit, pausing on the fake piercings. "What are you supposed to be, a pincushion?"

Dez gave Nash's gelled goldilocks a once-over right back, pausing on the tacky shark-tooth surfer necklace that hid a chip of the Alatyr stone. Dez smirked. "Better a pincushion than a washed-up boy band reject."

Nash barked out a surprised laugh as Dez stalked to his room to change. I was glad to see they'd officially entered the good-natured ribbing phase of team bonding.

Maybe Nash just needed some downtime to process the report. I tossed Nash an exterminator uniform. "You're up."

CHAPTER 36

Unfortunately, the trap door on Dez's package was a bust, and the frogs were stuck inside their box. "Now what?" I asked.

Going in without knowing what magical traps were waiting for me was a terrible idea. Without those frogs, Nash also couldn't get inside to install the thumb drive Dez needed to tap into the building's security feed. I'd be going in blind.

Dez pulled out a spare frog from his stash. "I could try again. Put a couple in another package."

I shook my head. "That's not going to work. Two deliveries from a courier on the same day would be too suspicious. We need to come up with another way to get one inside."

Nash held out his hands and Dez tossed him the frog. "You said they were waterproof, right?"

"Yeah."

Nash shoved the frog in his pocket and pointed to the exterminator logo on his chest. "We'll send the guy in the back door and listen for the scream when the witch spots it."

Dez frowned. "We can't just open the back door and toss a frog inside."

"That's not the kind of back door I'm talking about." Nash handed Dez his laptop. "Find me the sewer clean-out for her building."

I laughed when I realized how our little friend was going to make his appearance. "Tell me we can watch when Bellarose spots this in the toilet."

Dez grinned. "Get the snacks. We'll watch it on that big screen television like it's the Super Bowl."

I slapped him on the butt and ran to the kitchen for the leftover chips and salsa from lunch. Watching the all-powerful Zara Bellarose screech like a little kid when the tree frog hopped out of her toilet was the best thing I'd watched in years. My only regret was that I hadn't recorded it. That clip would have gone viral, for sure.

Thanks to Dez's wizardry, we were able to reroute Bellarose's frantic call for exterminator services to Nash's cellphone. Once he had an invitation, getting into her penthouse to install the thumb drive had been easy. Because Nash went in wired and with a hidden camera, we now had an audio sampling of Bellarose's voice and footage of the penthouse apartment as he walked through—both of which I might need to make it out of there in one piece. Instead of removing the spy frog, he hid it in a potted plant with a view of the living room and bathroom door. It wasn't perfect, but it would allow Dez to keep an eye on things.

While Dez cloned Bellarose's voice to produce a variety of common voice commands, I got dressed. This morning, Helen surprised me with a gift from home. Alyce had sewn me a custom designed cat burglar outfit that was amazing.

Naturally, it was made of all black matte material that

Helen had doused liberally with scent-blocker. The outfit included a built-in hip sheath for my dagger and rows of stretchy pockets down each leg that were the perfect size for potion bombs and tools of the trade. It also came with a matching nylon head covering that hid everything but my eyes, a pair of black touchscreen gloves, and soft-soled slip-on shoes that didn't make a sound as I walked.

The best part was the neck-to-navel hidden zipper that made stripping out of it when I needed to shift a breeze. I stuffed Isaac's cuff into the fanny pack I wasn't too ashamed to wear. I joined the others in the living room feeling like a ninja.

"Nice duds," Dez said, walking around me to get the three-sixty view.

Helen was too busy tidying up the place to give me more than a cursory glance, which was a sure sign that she was nervous. I took the empty chip bag from her hands and threw it away. "I'll be fine."

She waved a finger in my face. "Don't get cocky. Zara Bellarose is dangerous, and you're planning on tiptoeing around while she's there. Remember what I told you. She's a master illusionist. With her, you can't trust anything you see."

I patted the pockets that held Helen's various potion bombs. "Thanks to these, I'm well prepared. Nothing to worry about." I projected confidence to reassure her despite my pre-job jitters.

Helen didn't seem convinced, but at least she stopped cleaning.

I slid the silver and copper ring my mother made for me off my finger and held it out to Helen. "Can you keep this safe for me?"

"You know I will." She unhooked her necklace and

threaded the ring on the chain, so it lay on top of her iron spiral pendant.

"Let's run through it one more time," Nash insisted.

I humored him. "You'll pose as a rent-a-guard. Since the guards change shifts at eight o'clock, you'll incapacitate one of the three building guards before he makes it inside and hide him in the closed office building next door. I'll unlock the door before I go inside. The guard you'll intercept is a temp, so no one will be suspicious when you show up wearing his uniform. Once you're inside the control room, you'll give the verbal signal and run interference while Dez alters the security feed long enough for me to go in through the back. Then you'll stay on site until I'm out and give you the all clear. To get to the service elevator, I'll need to get past the facial and voice recognition on the door." I turned to Dez to find out how exactly we were accomplishing that.

He tossed me my cell phone. "I've added the audio clips to both of your phones in case you get separated. The first clip is Bellarose identifying herself. You'll need that to get into the building and to open the service entrance into the penthouse. Bellarose loves her tech, and many of her security features are also voice-activated. I've included some basic commands in case you need them."

"And you're sure the cloned voice will work?" Nash asked.

Dez nodded. "With AI, it's a near perfect imitation. It'll work."

"And the facial recognition?" Nash asked. We hadn't talked specifics yet about this part of the plan.

Dez grabbed a large envelope and held it up. "I told you it was unorthodox, but you'll have to trust me on this." He pulled out a high-definition paper photograph of Zara Bellarose's face.

Nash shot to his feet. "You've got to be kidding me. Some tech genius you are."

"Stick to your lane, G.I. Joe, and let me worry about mine." Dez slid the photo back in the envelope. "It sounds crazy, but it'll work. AI researchers tested it on everything from airport security to payment systems on three continents, and it worked for everything except systems that used light imaging, which this one does not."

I took the envelope. "If you say it'll work, then it's good enough for me."

Nash huffed but kept his opinion to himself.

"And the wards?" Helen asked. "Was your frog able to detect them?"

"Yup." Dez pulled up a drawing of the penthouse. "There are two wards you need to be aware of. One is here, barring entrance into her bedroom. The other is keyed to her walk-in panic room. I couldn't get a look inside since she didn't open it, but I suspect she keeps her personal stash of potions and relics inside."

That made sense. "No wards on the entrances though?"

"There's a tripwire ward on the front door that will alert her if anyone other than her guards enter. Because she has cleaners, food delivery, and an on-call masseuse, the service entrance is not warded, which makes it your access point." He pointed to the living room, which I'd have to pass through to get to the bathroom. "There's definitely magic in this room, but Helen's spell wasn't able to tell us what it does."

"That's where the magical booby traps will be," Helen said.

She was probably right. "If that's the case, I'll do my best to dodge them." If I stuck to the walls, I'd be less likely to set them off. "According to Bellarose's maid, the only time she takes off the cuff is when she showers. I'm timing it so

Bellarose will be taking her nightly shower when I arrive since it'll be much easier to snatch when it doesn't have its fangs buried in her wrist." *Thank goodness for disgruntled maids who loved to gossip, or I wouldn't have that tidbit.* "It's just a matter of slipping in, grabbing the artifact. Then I'll wait until Bellarose reaches for her towel and slap the magic-canceling handcuffs on her. Nash will be waiting for my signal to rappel in from the roof for her extraction."

We'd decided that leaving Bellarose loose on the premises was too big of a risk. With the magic-canceling handcuffs on her, she'd be no more dangerous than the average human. We'd stage a supernatural citizen's arrest and hand her over to the Enclave. Between the use of the cuff and the theft of the blood-tracing spell, Bellarose's days of running her stretch of the underground market would be over. The Enclave might even give us a bonus for her.

"And if things don't go to plan?" Helen asked.

I patted my trusty fanny pack. "Then I try Plan B."

We all took a collective breath, and then we got to work.

Nash was stunned when the paper mask actually got me into the building. We were all linked up with earpieces small enough to be undetectable but powerful enough to keep us in constant communication, which meant Dez could gloat about it working.

"I'm at the service elevator. Do you have eyes on her?" I asked.

"She's walking to the bathroom now," Dez said. "Give it ten seconds and then go."

While I counted it down, I pulled out Helen's incognito spell. I busted it open in my hands and rubbed it over my body. After wiping the spell dust on my pant leg, I put on my gloves. Then I cracked my knuckles, pulled down my mask, and hit the elevator button.

Everything about the penthouse was upscale from the zebra wood parquet floor throughout the great room to the elaborate metal sculpture on a pedestal in the entryway. It was minimalist to an extreme though, with only a few pieces of uncomfortable looking furniture in the massive room. A metal chandelier hung above a solid wood dining table, and a pair of twin cream-colored Italian leather armchairs sat near the oversized onyx fireplace along the back wall. Apparently, Zara Bellarose wasn't one for company.

I made my way to the great room and pressed my back to the wall. There was no time for nerves. I edged along the walls until I got to the bathroom and paused with my ear to the door. If I walked in before the shower steamed up, she'd definitely see the door open. Pulling this off required perfect timing.

The next thirty seconds passed with excruciating slowness. When I was sure the room was steamed over, I eased the door open and slipped inside. I could see the outline of the witch's body through the fogged-up shower door. She had her back to me, her head tipped back under the spray of the showerhead.

Although my heart hammered against my ribcage, I forced myself to move slowly. Incognito spell or not, sudden movement was likely to draw attention. The cuff was right where the maid said it would be—on the vanity across the room from the shower. I concentrated to keep my footsteps silent as I crossed the room. When I made it without incident, I picked up the golden serpent cuff and tucked it into my left pants pocket. From my right, I pulled out the magic-canceling handcuffs.

Zara Bellarose didn't give me time to put them on her. The sound of the shower door opening was the only warning I got before a dripping wet witch threw a spell at my head. *So much for being incognito.* The spell narrowly missed me when I hit the ground.

I picked up the only thing within reach and tossed it at

her. While she was dodging the trashcan, I ran for the door, digging out a potion ball as I went. My gloved hands were damp and stuck to the ants-in-your-pants spell, but I managed to hit her in the chest. I didn't wait around for her to retaliate. When I reached the doorway, I lobbed a flash bomb into the bathroom and slammed the door shut behind me. Not that a closed door would stop an angry witch.

"I'm compromised," I told the team, not bothering to keep my voice down. At this point, being quiet wasn't going to save me. "Nash, get to the extraction point. Dez, make sure Nash has a security-free route to the roof. And Helen, get the car ready." Helen had lobbied hard for a Camaro that could go from zero to sixty in five seconds. I'd vetoed it in favor of a classy Mercedes identical to the one Bellarose owned. I hoped I wouldn't regret bypassing that Camaro.

I had two routes through Bellarose's living room—the smart one or the fast one. I chose fast, hoping to dodge whatever magic was in the great room. Bad choice.

That parquet floor wasn't just for looks. A pressure plate activated the second I stepped on it. By the time I felt the slight give under my feet, it was too late. That pretty sculpture I'd admired earlier began to move, the metal layers rotating and opening like an eye. Then the real shit show started as it projected a wall of magical fire that spanned the entryway and blocked the exit. *I guess it's good I wasn't planning on going out the front door.*

I froze. Since I'd already triggered one magical booby trap, I wanted to avoid bumbling into another one. I studied the parquet pattern, looking for some sort of deviation that distinguished the pressure plates from the surrounding flooring.

"Riley, there are two guards at the service elevator," Dez

warned. "I cut the power to slow them down, but you'll need another way out."

"Little preoccupied right now."

"Go out through the window," Nash said. "Once I have Bellarose on the roof for pickup, I'll drop the line for you."

When I couldn't find any discernible difference in the floor pattern, I looked at the chandelier and wondered if it was sturdy enough to hold my weight. If I could reach it, maybe I could swing my body and leap for the wall.

Right on cue, Bellarose joined the party. She must have been confident I'd trigger her wall of magical fire because she'd taken the time to get dressed. As I watched, she flipped the first of three oversized switches on the wall next to her. Too late, I realized they were not ordinary light switches as bars slammed down over the windows.

"I don't think the window's going to work," I told the team. "Unless you can cut through metal bars, that is." I'd always wanted to try a jail break, but I hadn't imagined it would include an overpowered witch with a penchant for magical warfare. That seemed to lower the odds of success, considerably. After some creative swearing, Nash and Dez both said they were working on it.

I didn't have time to worry about the window, not with Bellarose eyeing me like the evening's entertainment. Since I couldn't afford distractions, I turned off my comm after warning my team I was going radio silent.

"Did you really think you could just tiptoe in here and take that cuff from me?" she asked. "Thank you for the advance warning though. Your little pickpocketing act with Isaac gave me plenty of time to prepare a little something for you."

"You realize I'm here on behalf of the Enclave, right?" I

asked on the slim chance I could talk myself out of here. "All they want is the artifact. Let me walk out of here with it, and you can go back to your busy life.

Her laugh was full-throated and husky, and the sound killed any hope of her seeing reason. "If you think they'll be satisfied with that artifact you took from me, you're more naïve than I thought." She cocked her head to the side as if considering how best to kill me. "Tell you what. If you make it through my gauntlet, I'll even let you walk out here with a parting gift. Of course, I'm going to have to take that demon relic back. I wouldn't want it to fall into the wrong hands."

She hit the second switch. The center of the floor where I stood dropped several feet. The six-foot section of floor all around me dropped even further until I was standing in the equivalent of an indoor pit surrounded by a parquet moat. I'd seen some secret safe rooms in my time, but this was some next-level home security right here. Rich people spent money on the craziest shit.

Thanks to my shifter genes, I boasted pretty impressive horizontal and vertical jumps. I might even be able to make it without needing to shift into my goat. Worse case, I'd twist an ankle if I miscalculated.

Bellarose seemed far too smug for there not to be another trick. "I've been chasing you for a long time. Let's see if you're as good as they say you are," she taunted.

Despite everything in me screaming to not look down, of course, I looked down. Hundreds of writhing bodies with eerie glowing eyes stared up at me. "I guess you have a thing for snakes, huh?" I called out.

Bellarose tilted her head and smiled. "They're magical you know. One touch of their venom will paralyze you, and they'll feast on your flesh and bone, so I don't have to deal with the cleanup. Isn't that clever?"

So freaking clever.

I eyed the distance again and decided not to risk it on two legs. I transferred the essentials from my outfit pockets to my trusty fanny pack. By the time I got everything in there, it was bulging. I put Bellarose's cuff in last, tucking it into the interior pocket to keep it separate from its mate. After peeling off my clothes, I put the strap of the pack between my teeth and shifted into my goat. I was sad to leave the outfit behind, but it was too big to fit in the pack. Besides, I had my emergency spandex shorts and tank top in there already. At least I wouldn't have to walk out of here naked.

"Your old alpha claimed you were a goat shifter, but since he was a double-crossing lowlife, I couldn't exactly take him at his word. But here you are," Bellarose called down.

Ignoring her weird commentary, I focused on the decision I needed to make. I could either go after Bellarose with the magic-canceling handcuffs in my pack, or I could open an escape route. Since I had both halves of the demon artifact in my possession, I chose the escape.

I made the leap easily, landing on the thin strip of flooring in front of the wall of magical fire blocking the front door. Shifting twice within minutes took its toll on my body, but I needed opposable thumbs for this next part, so I forced the shift. I quickly dressed in my spare clothes and pulled out the magic canceling handcuffs, tossing them into the mouth of the flames. They flickered out, leaving me a clear path to the door.

"Huh. I did not see that coming. I thought you'd try to walk right through it." Bellarose smiled indulgently before flipping the final switch before I could reach the door. A gossamer silver net dropped from the ceiling, pinning my body. That amount of silver would incapacitate—and eventually kill—any other shifter. Just because the silver didn't burn my skin didn't make fighting my way out of it any easier. I crawled from under the net, my body shaking with the effort. But it took too long. Bellarose was there before I could get to my feet.

She bent down beside me and ran a finger across my cheek. "All that silver and not a single burn on you. Remarkable," she mused. She held out her hand. "Now hand over my artifact, and I'll give you that parting gift."

I let my shoulders sag in defeat before pulling the pack from beneath my body and reaching inside. I handed her Isaac's cuff and hoped she didn't look at it too closely. Bellarose was high enough on her victory that she put it on her wrist without examining it.

Once it was safely on her wrist, she grabbed my head with both hands and began to chant. The pain was enough to make spots dance in my vision. I felt her inside my head the same way I'd felt Isaac when we'd performed the blood magic memory spell together. This time was worse though, as if she cracked something in my head wide open and power flooded in. She bent down beside me.

"Do you see it now? The magic?"

The last thing I saw before the magic overwhelmed me was Zara Bellarose leaning over me. It was as if I'd lived my entire life watching black and white television, and I got my first glimpse of color. Magic pulsed all around me. It was in the bodies of the snakes still crawling below us, in the wards I could now see, and in the residue of the potion bombs and the spells Bellarose had cast.

"What did you do to me?" I rasped.

"I made you whole to prepare you for what's coming." She stood up to leave.

Despite the disorientation, I got my hand inside the zippered pocket in my pack that held Valac's cuff. "Stop," I ordered the second it was on my wrist.

Like a marionette, Bellarose stopped abruptly and waited for instruction. I shivered, not enjoying the feel of controlling another even if it were a necessary evil. I flipped the switches on the wall until the room returned to normal. Then I turned my comm back on and arranged for extraction.

Nash took Bellarose up to the roof first and came back for me while Dez stood guard over her. By the time I scrambled over the side of the building onto the roof, the sound of helicopter wings greeted me.

"I called Volkov, and he arranged for the Enclave to pick her up, so we didn't have to transport a volatile witch," Nash said, before I could ask.

"Good thinking." I'd spent as much time in Zara Bellarose's company as I could stand.

Sato leapt from the helicopter and landed as gracefully as a cat. He took possession of both Bellarose and the cuff on my wrist without fanfare. As Sato led her away, I was still reeling from the effects of the magical hangover. When I swayed, Nash's arm was there to brace me, and my gaze landed on the shark tooth necklace. I took a step toward Bellarose as they neared the waiting chopper.

"Wait," I called after them.

Sato paused with an impatient frown. "I'll wire the money," he said. "But we need to go."

This wasn't about the money. It was about closure.

"Why were you after the Alatyr stone?" I yelled loud enough for my voice to carry.

Bellarose didn't turn around, but she answered. "It was never the stone I was after."

They were gone before I could ask any more questions.

CHAPTER 38

Now that I'd handed over the cuffs of Valac, we were left to celebrate our first successful job as a team. Although Luca Cardelli was still in the wind, the Enclave had taken both Zara Bellarose and Isaac off our hands. More importantly, Sato had wired the remainder of our fee and expenses into my account yesterday.

After a couple days of rest and recuperation, I was waiting to meet my team outside a dilapidated warehouse in West Bottoms. Four stories tall, the red-brick warehouse had seen better days. Several windows were busted out, and the ones that weren't had a layer of grime over them from years of disuse. The building had a small side entrance with a home-made flier taped to it and a huge bay door to a loading dock once used by the textile manufacturer that had operated out of this building. Like many old buildings in West Bottoms, it had more character than purpose.

I was practically vibrating with excitement. I checked my watch—five minutes until the meetup time I'd sent out yesterday via group text. Although everyone grumbled about my frequent use of the group chat, it was an efficient way to guilt people into showing up for my debrief. I checked my pocket to make sure I still had the envelopes tucked inside.

Volkov showed up first. He eyed the building suspiciously. "Isn't this where you and Kali got tattoos from that sketchy tattoo guy?"

"Dingo is long gone," I assured him, rubbing the sepia goat head tattoo on the inside of my wrist.

"Hey," Kali called as she and Craig joined us. "I'm not getting another tattoo."

I didn't blame her since the first one was kind of a disaster. "That's not why we're meeting here," I promised.

I refused to say any more until Nash, Dez, and Helen arrived. My other witches were busy running the Stitch Witch, but I promised to show them the surprise after they closed up the shop tonight.

"Is everyone ready?" I asked as Nash finally joined us, surveying the building behind me with a scowl.

Their nods were less enthusiastic than I would have liked, but once they saw the surprise, they'd warm up. When the bay door got stuck, Volkov grabbed the handle from me and muscled it the rest of the way open. I beamed at him before ducking inside.

I let everyone check out the cavernous first floor before leading the way to the back staircase like a tour guide. "This way," I called.

"I don't think these stairs are safe, Riley" Volkov said, testing the bottom one with his weight.

I turned around to face them and bounced on the stair I stood on. "Completely safe," I declared. Thankfully, it didn't crack. Based on my last visit here, it could've gone either way. I ignored their grumbling about death traps and sprinted up the stairs. When I reached the top, I spread my arms and blocked the doorway to the fourth floor.

"Okay, before we go in, I have something for you guys." I pulled out envelopes for Dez and Nash with their cuts and ones for Kali and Helen that were stuffed with gift cards since both of them refused to take actual money for their services. Because I didn't want Volkov or Craig to feel left out, I bought them each an over-priced thank you card. "I want you all to know how much it means to me that you showed up—today and on the job when it mattered most." I had a better speech prepared, but I'd never been great at keeping surprises. Two days, and I was past my limit. I threw open the door and led the way inside.

This room was in even worse shape than the first floor. The worn plank floors were mostly intact, except for the corner I'd blocked off with a roll of police tape I found downstairs. And the walls could definitely use a fresh coat of paint. But I didn't see any of that when I spun in a circle and waited for everyone's reaction.

Dez and Nash exchanged confused looks. "What is this place?" Dez asked.

"It's our new headquarters. Surprise!" I screamed.

"Um," Nash said.

"Like for the job?" Dez asked, looking around wide eyed.

Volkov and Craig stood off to the side, their expressions carefully neutral.

"Yes, for the job," I said. "I used my cut to negotiate a great rate and paid for the year in advance."

Helen poked a dead rat with the toe of her orthopedic sneaker. "How good was this deal, hon?"

"Thirty-five thousand dollars," I said. "For the whole

thing!" I did a little I'm-winning-at-life dance while they all stared at me.

Volkov made a strangled sound, but when I looked at him, his expression was unreadable. "Does that include renovations?" he asked carefully.

"Nah, but I like DIY projects," I said. "It'll be like team building."

When I was met with silence, my enthusiasm took a direct hit.

Kali broke the silence. She took a good look around and declared it a space with great potential. "A little cheerful paint and a throw rug, and this will be amazing," she promised.

It was enough to snap everyone else out of their shock, and they milled around checking out the room. Volkov stilled when he spotted the only new thing in the room—a giant gray sectional with reclining seats and stain guard.

"You bought your couch," he said, a catch in his voice. "For your headquarters."

"I did."

Volkov caught my hand and pulled me into his body. He cupped the back of my head and kissed me until I forgot we had an audience.

It took the sound of multiple people clearing their throats to break the moment.

"About damn time," Helen said as we broke apart. "If you would've waited any longer to make your move, pup, you would've cost me a hundred bucks."

"You all bet on me?" I squealed.

"Just the girls and I." Helen said, her grin absolutely unrepentant. "Now. You young'uns can get to work, and I'll be back in a week to check on the progress." She gave me a passing pat on the shoulder. "I can't leave Bea unsupervised for too long. You did good, hon. I'm proud of you."

I crossed the room to where Dez and Nash stood awkwardly not talking to one another. "What's the verdict?" I asked Dez, biting my lip. "Are we a team, or what?"

Dez looked at Nash with a loud sigh. "I suppose he's passed the interview, although I have some notes."

Nash flipped him off. Then he wandered over to an empty corner. "You know, this would make a great spot for a bird cage."

"Maybe we could build a big one for when you bring Garth to work," I conceded.

We spent the next twenty minutes plotting the renovation and thirty minutes after that trying to make sense of Bellarose's parting gift to me. The magical rebound headache was gone, but I'd spent the past two days sequestered with Helen and the girls trying to figure out what it all meant. We'd searched through grimoires and tomes on magic without luck. We couldn't find a single mention of a shifter with any kind of magical ability. I was still immune to alpha commands and vampire compulsions. We'd tested both. And while I could now sense wards, they seemed to have no effect on me. We'd tested that, too. All we knew for certain was that I could now sense magic.

Our current working theory was that there was a witch descendent lurking somewhere in my family tree, despite its improbability. Without any records of my parents, I had no way to even begin looking into my ancestors. However, even if a witch did turn up in my family tree, it didn't explain it. As far as we knew, in a pairing between a shifter and a witch, the shifter ability always repressed any elemental magic.

When I finished updating everyone on what we'd learned,

Craig handed me a letter-sized envelope. "What's this?" I asked.

"The DNA results Volkov asked me to run on your mother's hair sample and the one you submitted came back this morning," Craig said.

The envelope was unopened. Everyone crowded around as I broke the seal. I took a deep breath and pulled out the results. I should have been prepared, but I wasn't. My mother's real name was Amelia Hunt, and her DNA was not that of a shifter nor of a witch. According to the test results, Amelia Hunt had been one hundred percent human.

And she shared none of that DNA with me.

Don't miss Riley's next adventure in *Magic Heist*.

Order

If you enjoyed this book, please consider leaving a review or rating on Amazon and/or Goodreads. Your reviews help new readers discover my books and are always appreciated!

If you'd like to be notified of new releases and exclusive content, you can sign up for my newsletter at lamcbride.com/newsletter/ and join my Facebook Readers Group at https://www.facebook.com/groups/lamcbridereaders

ALSO BY L.A. MCBRIDE

*Each series can be read independently, but they are set in the same world
with some character crossover.*

KALI JAMES SERIES

Book 1: Fastening the Grave

Book 2: Threading the Bones

Book 3: Stitching the Talisman

Book 4: Gathering the Dead

RILEY CRUZ SERIES

Prequel: Boneyard Thief

Book 1: Relic Hunter

Book 2: Brimstone Burglar

Book 3: Magic Heist

ACKNOWLEDGMENTS

Special thanks to my husband who is my biggest cheerleader. Thank you also goes to my amazing editor Sara who helps me craft a better story. I'm grateful for my fabulous ARC team who helps catch those pesky errors that slip past and spreads the Riley love. The biggest thank you goes to my readers, who patiently waited for this story.